A VERY MERRY MOVIE IN PINE RIDGE

A HOCKEY HEARTS MM HOLIDAY ROMANCE

JEFF ADAMS

A Very *Merry Movie* in Pine Ridge

JEFF ADAMS

ONE

August

THE ENGINE of my truck was the only sound on the last stretch of highway winding into Pine Ridge.

I rolled the window down, and warm July air rushed in, thick with the aroma of Douglas fir. The same sharp scent greeted me every summer and told me I was finally home.

Up ahead, the Cascades sawed at the blue sky, their familiar jagged lines a constant in the skyline of Pine Ridge.

The off-season should've been my time to decompress. A few months to let the bruises fade, the aches settle, and the pressure of an NHL season to recede.

Six weeks had passed since the conference finals —a brutal game 7 overtime loss. Coach had called it "a hell of a run," but the disappointment of coming that close for the first time in three seasons still lingered.

I'd spend the next couple of months here, except for two weeks when I'd head to Vermont to work with teens at a hockey camp.

Outside of that trip, I'd spend time with my sister and niece, work in our store, and re-connect with the hometown I loved. But this summer brought unwanted pressure, and something exciting vying for my attention in Pine Ridge too.

I made the last turn onto Main Street, and my foot eased off the gas. It was like driving into a snow globe someone had shaken and then dropped into the wrong season.

Garlands of faux pine and glittering red ribbon were draped from every lamppost. Wreaths with plastic holly adorned the doors of the hardware store and the bakery. Storefronts glowed beneath rows of lights strung in bright crisscrosses above the awnings.

In the town square, a crew of people in headsets swarmed around the gazebo, its roof dusted with a layer of what looked like powdered sugar. A half-decorated Christmas tree stood next to the gazebo as someone struggled to untangle lights.

Christmas in July.

Paige had sent pictures when the transformation began last week, but seeing it in person was another thing altogether.

I couldn't help the jolt of joy at the sight of it all. I had a weakness for Christmas movies—the more romantic the better. After rough games, when my body was one massive ache, nothing beat sinking into the couch with a cup of something warm and watching some big-city lawyer fall for a small-town bookstore owner.

The fact that my friend Shawn wrote this movie made it even better. I couldn't wait to see him. Hopefully he'd give me an insider's peek behind the scenes since he'd also been teasing me with pictures for days.

I pulled into the angled parking spot in front of Reeve's Textiles, the space my mom had claimed as her own for forty years. The brick facade was the same deep red I'd known my entire life, the gold-leaf lettering on the window—Reeve's Textiles, Est. 1923 —faded but proud. It was more than a building.

Five generations of sweat and determination built this place.

And it was in trouble.

The bell above the door chimed, a familiar, cheerful sound clashing with the tension in my shoulders. The store smelled as it always had: cedar from the display shelves, mixed with the vanilla potpourri we had on a low simmer by the coffee station. That aroma pulled me straight back to childhood, of hiding in forts built from bolts of fabric, and learning to count by sorting buttons with my grandmother.

My gaze drifted to the far wall, where a small sign marked "Local Artisans" hung above a display of handcrafted items. Among them were my framed embroidery pieces, signed with the simple initials "A.R." Most of the town knew those were mine, but no one made a big deal out of it. My aunt Rose taught me needlework when I was young, and it had become my meditation away from the intensity of hockey.

Paige stood behind the massive, worn cutting table that dominated the center of the space. Her brown hair, pulled back in a messy knot, framed the faint shadows under her eyes that hadn't been there when we'd seen each other a few months ago when she came to my game in Seattle. She folded a length of deep blue merino wool with careful, almost robotic precision.

She looked up and smiled. "Augie! It's good to have you home."

"Paigey." I closed the distance and wrapped her in a hug. She hugged me back as I lifted her and twirled her like I'd done from the time I'd become taller than her.

"How was the drive?" She returned to her folding. We both had the skill to work and keep up a conversation.

"Long. Traffic was a beast coming out of Seattle."

I leaned against the table and took in the store. It was quiet for a Tuesday afternoon. A couple of tourists browsed the yarn section, their voices a low murmur, but otherwise, it was just us. "So, this movie thing is really something."

Paige snorted, shooting me a look long enough to roll her eyes. "It's a circus. It's only been a week of setup, and half the town's complaining about the parking. Meanwhile, the other half is trying to get cast as an extra."

"Shawn's been blowing up my phone with pics," I said with a grin.

"And you?" She gave me a knowing look. "I bet the NHL's toughest right wing is thrilled to see how Christmas movies get made."

"No idea what you're talking about." I fought a grin and failed. "Just curiosity about what they're doing to our town."

"Uncle Augie!" Paige's ten-year-old daughter, Rose, came running up from the back of the shop.

"There she is." I squatted down and opened my arms. She crashed into me and wrapped her arms around my neck.

"It's about time you got here. Did you see all the movie stuff?"

"I did." I relaxed as I hugged her. It was impossible to be stressed with Rose, who always had a sunny disposition. Or at least she did that for me. I knew from Paige that Rose could be stubborn when she wanted to be. It was one of the ways she was like the aunt she'd been named for. "Should we go exploring and see what's going on?"

"I've been doing that for the last few days," she said as if she expected me to know that. "I can take you around to all the good stuff though?"

"I'd love that."

She bounced with excitement as I released her. "Let's go!"

"Let Augie catch his breath a minute." Paige interceded as she poured coffee into our mugs. "Besides, I bet you haven't finished your chores yet."

Rose made a face but didn't argue. "Fine." She drew out the word. "I'll finish. When he's done with his coffee, we can go. Okay?" She looked between us.

My only response was to look at Paige. I learned

a long time ago not to get between mother and daughter.

"Okay," Paige said.

"Yay!" Rose took off.

Paige and I shared a smile, and she shook her head. "She's been so excited for you to get here for all the movie stuff. Between that and the filming that's going to happen here, she's hyped up as if she's had too much Halloween candy."

"I bet. It's not everyday you see something like what's going on out there."

She passed me a cup, and I blew across the surface of the hot beverage.

"So, what's the update?" I asked, my voice low so Rose and our shoppers wouldn't overhear.

She added milk and sugar to her coffee from the cart that sat next to the cutting table. We'd offered customers coffee for as long as I could remember. This table had seen all kinds of conversations over the years.

"He made offers yesterday afternoon." Her voice came out flat as she turned around, wool folding temporarily forgotten. "For the whole block. From the corner up to the movie theater."

"Donovan made an offer?" The name was foul in my mouth. Corbin Donovan. A developer from

Seattle with a portfolio of glass-and-steel monstrosities and a smile that always felt a little sinister.

We'd been hearing about his reputation and whispers about what he wanted to do for a year. The phantom threat had suddenly become very real.

"I told you about that town hall meeting he spoke at two weeks ago. Slick presentation, fancy renderings of a *revitalized Pine Ridge*. Patios, valet parking, a luxury spa. He made it sound like he was doing us a favor."

"And people bought it?" The hot twist of anger in my gut stabbed at me every time we had to talk about Donovan's latest move. It was the same fire that made me effective on the ice.

"Some did. The ones who are tired of struggling. He said the offers would be good, and he wasn't kidding. We got one way over market value. For people like the Millers at the bakery, who are barely breaking even... it's tempting. Donovan's already painting anyone who wants to stay as obstacles to progress."

"Downtown is the heart of Pine Ridge." The words came out sharper than I'd intended. Paige didn't need convincing.

"The heart's having a coronary," she said before taking a drink of her coffee. "You know, it's been two bad winters in a row. Not enough snow for good skiing, so not enough tourists. Online retailers are eating some businesses alive. The location fee from this movie is a nice bonus, but it's only a bandage for most. Not everyone has a family member who makes excellent money and invests back into the business."

She took my hand and squeezed it. I'd been *investing* for a few years to make sure the staff stayed paid, the bills got covered, and the store ran with the kind of quality our parents and grandparents would be proud of.

Helping financially was the least I could do when I wasn't here working beside Paige.

I hated feeling helpless. On the ice, I always knew what to do. Outwork. Outskate. Outshoot. Do what the coaches said. Trust your teammates. Take the shot when it's there.

This was different. I couldn't check this problem into the boards to stop it.

"So what's the number?" I asked. "What's he offering us?"

The figure she said made my breath catch. With that much money on the table, I understood why some might want to sell.

Except that's not what we wanted. The store was our family's legacy. One I wanted to come back to when I retired from the NHL. Paige and I didn't want to be the last generation for Reeve's Textiles.

"And if we say no?" I asked, even though I knew the answer.

"He's giving everyone until the movie wraps. He's got a couple of council members in his pocket, so who knows what he might be able to do."

I stood up and started pacing, the space between the cutting table and the quilt rack feeling too small. "Let me see what I can do. I'll talk to my agent and find out if they can recommend a lawyer to take a look. I can..."

It was the wrong thing to say. Her expression hardened.

"This isn't a problem your NHL money and connections can fix, August." Her voice dropped, the edge of annoyance sharpening her words. "This isn't about one store. It's about the whole of downtown. You can't just buy the whole block. And even if you could, what right do you have to tell others they can't sell just because we have a lifeline to weather the ups and downs? And... maybe I need a break, too. Even though we're surviving, watching the struggle is tough."

The shot landed, direct and painful. My connection to this place ran deep, anchored in memory and a hope for the future, but hers was in the here and now. I wondered if she hadn't always been truthful with me when I asked how she was doing.

We'd agreed years ago, when I got drafted, that she would handle the store on her own once our parents retired. She'd even doubled down on that after her divorce, making it clear she wanted to raise Rose in Pine Ridge and keep running the store.

For me, I had six or seven years left. Maybe I'd get a few more if I was lucky. Then, my plan was to retire here, work at the store and probably coach locally.

"I'm sorry." I rubbed the back of my neck.

"No. Don't be." Her shoulders slumped. "I'm just... tired. This guy Donovan, he walks in here with his thousand-dollar suit and his condescending smile, talking about maximizing assets, and he looks at this place..." She gestured out at the store. "And he sees nothing. Only a building to tear down."

I squeezed the bridge of my nose, the familiar prelude to a headache starting behind my eyes. Her exhaustion. Everyone's anxiety. A century of family history pressed down on me. I was the local boy who made good. The town's success story. I should be able to fix this. But Paige was right. My money couldn't solve this one.

"Okay," I said, my voice steady again. "We're not giving up. We fight. We organize the other owners who want to stay. We find a way."

Paige's smile was tired, but kind. "There's the team captain. Always got a pep talk ready."

"It's not a pep talk. It's a plan."

"It's a start," she corrected gently. "I'm glad you're home, Augie. These next few weeks are going to be tough." She came around the table and gave me another hug, this one longer. "Now, make yourself useful and help me unload the new shipment of alpaca blend before Rose takes you on her tour."

We worked in comfortable silence for the next half hour, hauling boxes and stocking shelves. The rhythm came easily—one we'd shared since we were kids. For a little while, I could pretend nothing had changed.

When we finished, Rose declared it was time to go. I said goodbye to Paige, promising to come over for dinner the next night, and stepped back out onto Main Street.

The late-afternoon sun cast long shadows. The Christmas decorations looked so out of place in the summer light and with the mid-July warmth. A string of lights draped across the entrance to my family's store cast a festive, multicolored glow on the worn brick.

Rose talked a mile a minute about the movie, the decorations, the actors she'd seen, and the equipment scattered around town.

Paige had called the movie a bandage. A circus. I looked at the tinsel, plastic holly, and the ridiculous snowbanks that weren't melting. How could something so fake be any kind of fix to save something so real?

After all, real life didn't work like a Christmas movie.

TWO

Landon

My world was a rectangle. Twenty-four frames per second of curated reality, and at this moment, my reality was being ruined by a patch of stubbornly green grass.

"Can we get more snow on that grass?" I called out, my eye still pressed to the viewfinder. "It looks like a putting green with dandruff. We need a blanket of fresh-fallen snow, not a light dusting."

Felix, my producer, sighed audibly beside me. It was a sound I'd come to know well over the last eight years. That sigh said, "I know, but honestly, Landon…" without him uttering a single word.

"It's ninety-two degrees, Lan." He wiped a sheen of sweat from his forehead with the back of his hand.

He juggled his tablet and a bottle of water. "We're doing the best we can. We'll get some of the white fabric down so the green can't show through."

"That works." I stepped back from the camera, breaking the spell. The real world rushed in, a jarring mess of extension cords, frazzled-looking production assistants in shorts, and the oppressive July sun beating down on Main Street. The manufactured Christmas cheer felt absurd. A plastic snowman looked like it was sweating.

I knew Christmas movies were made like this, but it was my first time experiencing it. I was here to make holiday magic, and that meant not letting the seams show.

This was day three of a fourteen-day shoot, and my eighth straight day in Pine Ridge. We had a budget of two million dollars to create 90 minutes of predictable, heartwarming, and highly marketable holiday romance.

Deliver *Christmas in the Cascades* on time and on budget, and I would finally get to make *Silo*. My film. A gritty, monochrome character study about isolation during the Dust Bowl that is also a commentary about the present day and how people can be surrounded by everything and still be utterly alone. That was the deal I'd made with Ted Vance, the studio head who owed me a favor. He got his profitable holiday movie, and I got my shot at art.

"Declan is wandering out of his light again." I pinched the bridge of my nose. "And he's slouching. He's supposed to be the town's beloved hockey hero, not a teenager waiting for the bus."

"Let me talk to him." Felix's voice was the calm compared to my serrated-edge focus. "Give the kid a break. He's used to green screens and alien invasions, not heartfelt chats by a gazebo."

I watched Declan Thorne, our leading man, check his phone, brow furrowed. His performance hit its marks, but seemed completely lost without a CGI monster to react to. He should've been gazing wistfully at the town's Christmas tree, a massive spruce a dozen people had spent six hours decorating. Instead, he came off as if he was trying to remember his grocery list.

"This scene is the heart of the first act," I muttered, more to myself than to Felix. "He leaves the city, he's heartbroken, he arrives in this charming town... and he feels a flicker of hope. I need that on his face. Not... whatever that is."

"We'll get it," he promised. "We always get it."

It was his standard reassurance, dating back to our first project together—a series of sports commercials with an impossible timeline. Felix had pulled it off, and ever since, he'd been my buffer against the on-set chaos. He was the only person I allowed close enough to know what went on inside my head.

A drop of sweat traced a path from my hairline down my temple. The heat pressed in, thicker and more suffocating than forecast. Just one more challenge we couldn't control. My black t-shirt, part of the uniform I'd maintained since college, had been a poor choice for this climate. Unfortunately, it was the only thing I'd packed.

Before I could respond, a shadow fell over us. I looked up, my eyes narrowing. A man in a suit that cost more than my first car stood there, a leather briefcase in one hand. His smile was all polished veneers and condescension. He looked as out of place here as a shark in a koi pond. And somehow, he wasn't sweating.

"Gentlemen," he said, his voice smooth as scotch. "Quite the operation you have here. I'm Corbin Donovan. My associates and I are working on a revitalization project for downtown."

Donovan. I remembered the name from some dry production email about local permits. I didn't care. He was another variable in the equation I was trying to simplify.

"We have all the necessary permits, signed off by

the mayor," Felix said immediately, stepping slightly in front of me as he always did when a civilian approached.

"Oh, I'm sure you do." Donovan's eyes scanned our mountain of equipment with a dismissive air. "I'm just curious about the timeline. This disruption to local business... it can't go on indefinitely."

I felt a hot spike of irritation. Disruption. I was bringing a production to his one-horse town that infused capital between the permits, location fees, and the cast and crew staying in town. This wasn't a disruption. It was a goddamn gift.

"We wrap in eleven days." My tone was flat and dismissive. I turned to my director of photography. "Jen, let's swap to the 50mm for the close-up. I want the background to fall off, just a bokeh of twinkly lights. Let's make him look like he's in a snow globe."

Donovan's smile tightened. I'd effectively ended the conversation without acknowledging him further.

Good.

He gave a stiff nod. "Well. Enjoy your movie." He turned and walked away, his expensive shoes clicking on the hot pavement.

"Charming," Felix muttered, watching him go.

"He's irrelevant." I looked through the camera

again. The world snapped back into its perfect, controllable rectangle. "The snow looks good. Let's do this. Places, please!"

THE DAY STRETCHED ON, a series of battles against the forces threatening to derail my vision. Heat continued to cause trouble. Local extras missed their marks. And Declan Thorne continued to manifest all the emotional depth of a cardboard cutout. I pushed through it all with the singular focus that earned me fear from new crewmembers and grudging respect from those who'd worked with me before.

As the sun began to sink, casting long golden rectangles across Main Street, I called it.

"That's a wrap for today. Review dailies in twenty."

The crew, accustomed to my abrupt transitions, started the practiced dance of breaking down equipment. I stood for a moment, my shoulders tight with tension, watching the chaotic beauty of it. This was the only kind of family I'd allowed myself since Thomas had walked out three years ago, taking with him the naïve notion that love and ambition could coexist.

"You need to eat something." Felix appeared at my side. "I had craft services save you a plate."

"After dailies." My focus was already shifting to the next task waiting in my trailer.

"You said that yesterday, and then you didn't have a bite." Felix matched my stride, his tone light but insistent. "This is me fulfilling my contractual obligation to keep you alive through principal photography."

I rolled my eyes but gave him a begrudging half-smile. "Fine. Bring the food with you."

The air conditioning in my trailer hit like a physical blow, raising goosebumps on my damp skin. I sank into the chair at my small desk, the familiar ache in my lower back a constant companion during shoots. An organized grid of storyboards, shot lists, and a color-coded schedule covered the wall opposite me.

My script for *Silo* sat on the corner of the workspace, its cover page already showing wear from my constant handling. I opened it, flipping to Scene 72—the heart of the film, where my stoic, isolated farmer breaks down. It was still not right. The dialogue felt stilted, with the emotion manufactured. I'd been stuck on it for months, unable to access the raw vulnerability the moment demanded. It was an unrelenting reminder of my creative limitations.

A knock at the door broke my concentration. Felix entered without waiting for a response, a plate of food in one hand and his ever-present tablet in the other.

"Eat." He sat the plate down. "And while you do that, we need to talk about tomorrow's location scout at Reeve's Textiles."

I took a bite of cold pasta salad. "I already did the initial walkthrough with the art department. It's fine. What's there to discuss?"

He swiped through his tablet, pulling up a set of photos. "The owners. Specifically, the brother."

"August Reeve. The hockey player."

"Not just any hockey player." Felix showed me a photo of a broad-shouldered man in a Denver Mountaineers jersey. "Two-time All-Star. Hometown hero. And very protective of his family's store. The location manager met him today and says he can be... difficult."

I studied the image. August Reeve looked solid, immovable. His eyes held the calm confidence of someone accustomed to getting his way through sheer physical presence.

A jock with a territorial streak. Perfect.

"Wonderful." I pushed the half-eaten food away. "So I have to babysit a prima donna athlete with a small-town hero complex. Because clearly my life wasn't complicated enough."

"Just be your usual charming self," Felix quipped, collecting the plate. "I'm sure that will go over splendidly with the local celebrity."

"Don't need him to like me." I turned back to my storyboards. "Just need to use his precious shop for a day."

Felix paused at the door, his expression softening into something dangerously close to concern. "You know, Lan, you could try a different approach. Not everyone responds well to the imperious director act."

"It's not an act," I countered, not looking up. "It's efficiency."

"It's a wall," Felix said quietly. "And one of these days, someone's going to climb over it."

I didn't respond. He sighed, once again saying everything he needed to.

Once he left, I stared at the chaos of my production board, the careful grid that represented the only thing that mattered. Felix's words hung in the air, an unwelcome truth. It was a wall. One I'd been building since Thomas had stood in our apartment, suitcase in hand, and told me we were done.

"Your career will always come first," he'd said,

voice bitter with disappointment. "You don't want a partner. You want a production assistant. Someone to manage the mundane details while you focus on your cinematic vision."

He hadn't been wrong. I'd chosen *Silo* over him. And in the three years since, I'd turned that choice into a doctrine. Any relationships that weren't professional ones were liabilities. The work was the only thing that mattered.

I pushed the memory away. Tomorrow I'd meet August Reeve, another complication to control. I would charm him, or intimidate him, or whatever it took to get what I needed from his store. And then I would move on to whatever came next.

Sitting down at the desk, I opened my laptop and pulled up the photos of Reeve's Textiles, studying the angles, planning my shots, trying to see the story that could be told in this storefront.

It was a century-old shop, full of history and texture. Good bones, as they said in the business. But it would need work. The lighting was all wrong. The layout screamed chaos, but I could picture how to transform it from a lived-in space into the perfect frame for a meet-cute.

A knock at the door interrupted my thoughts. Felix spoke as he entered, "We're ready to go on dailies." The DP, the editor, and the art director followed him inside.

Time to for the tedious but necessary ritual of dissecting the day's footage. It was an excellent distraction from thinking about what obstacles August Reeve might throw at me tomorrow.

THREE

August

Paige and I were behind the counter, a comfortable quiet between us as she worked on the store's schedule and I sorted through a jar of mismatched vintage buttons. Since I was a kid, this was a task I'd found satisfying. Each button was a small piece of history: pearlescent discs from a grandmother's cardigan, heavy brass from a grandfather's coat.

"Remember Mrs. Gable?" I held up a chipped, flower-shaped button. "She had a dress covered in these."

Paige smiled without looking up from her laptop. "She made you cookies every time you helped carry her bags out. You always came back with chocolate on your face."

"They were good cookies."

"Cookies that you'd eat before you got back here." She glanced at me and winked.

It was moments like this I missed most when I was in Denver. The simple rhythm of being home, the shared history that didn't need explaining. For a little while, I could almost forget the Donovan problem and that he wanted to destroy all of this.

The cheerful chime of the bell above the door cut through the quiet. I looked up, expecting another tourist or maybe Mrs. Henderson from down the street.

It wasn't.

Two men walked in, and they were clearly not from Pine Ridge. The first was a little older, with a harried but kind look on his face, carrying a tablet like it held the most valuable information in it. The second man was the one who pulled all the air out of the room.

He was lean and wiry, dressed in black from his t-shirt to his ridiculously clean designer sneakers. His dark hair was perfectly, intentionally messy. He moved with an intensity, his sharp blue eyes scanning the store not with the wonder of a customer, but with the critical gaze of a tax auditor. He was assessing, judging, cataloging. This had to be the director.

The customers browsing yarn glanced up, their conversations faltering as the director's presence seemed to disrupt the energy in the shop. A middle-aged woman nudged her friend, whispering something that made them both steal another glance. Rose, who'd been dusting items in the local artisans section, stared.

The man in black stopped in the middle of the store, one hand on his hip, and did a slow, three-hundred-and-sixty-degree turn.

"The bones are good." His voice was crisp and filled the quiet space. It was a voice used to giving commands. "Great texture on the wood. The natural light from these front windows is soft, but we'll need to augment it. And those overhead fluorescents. They're hideous. They have to go."

My hand tightened around a small, porcelain button. Hideous? Our parents had installed those lights fifteen years ago because the old ones hummed.

I placed the button carefully back in the jar, trying to control the flare of irritation.

Paige closed her laptop with a soft click. "Can I help you?" Her voice was polite but cool.

The man's focus snapped to us. His eyes, an impossible shade of blue, flickered from Paige to me, lingering for a fraction of a second too long. I felt a strange jolt, like a static shock, and immediately pushed it away.

The guy with the tablet stepped forward with an apologetic smile. "I'm Felix Barlow, producer of *Christmas in the Cascades,* and this is Landon Winslow, the director. We're here for the final location walkthrough."

"Right." Paige's tone didn't warm. "We weren't expecting you today."

She and I came around the corner as Winslow took a few steps closer. His gaze swept over the counter, the antique cash register, and the wall of cubbies behind us filled with colorful skeins of yarn.

As he moved, he nearly collided with a customer who carried an armful of fabric. I lunged forward, catching a bolt of felt just as it slipped from her grasp.

"Oh my goodness, thank you, August," the woman said, flustered.

"You're welcome, Mrs. Albert." I gathered the rest of the things she had. "Let me take these to the register for you."

I glanced at Winslow, expecting some acknowledgment of the near disaster, but his attention had already moved on.

His hands formed a frame in front of his eyes. "This all feels a little cluttered for the shot I have in mind. We'll need to clear this main counter. And that rack of quilts is blocking the sightline to the back of the store. It has to go."

This guy treated a century of my family's work as if it were a messy closet someone hired him to clean out. My grandfather built the wooden quilt rack the summer before I was born. I could still remember him showing me how to sand joints when I was seven, his callused hands guiding mine over the grain of the wood. "Always with the grain, Augie," he'd say. "That's how you honor what the tree was meant to be."

Paige's expression was hardening, and I knew her patience, already worn thin, was about to snap. I stepped forward to handle the situation.

"That rack was built by our grandfather," I said, keeping my voice even. "It stays."

Winslow's intense gaze swiveled to me. For the first time, he was actually looking at me, not just past me. There was a mix of surprise and annoyance in his expression. He looked me over from my face, down my chest, to my hands resting on the worn wood of the cutting table, then back up. It was a slow, deliberate appraisal that sent a shiver down my spine.

"You must be the brother." It wasn't a question. "August Reeve."

"That's right."

"The screenplay writer's a fan," he added.

What was that supposed to mean?

I watched as he surveyed the store again, this time landing on the local artisans' wall next to the quilt rack.

"I need a clean shot." His voice was back to clipped and professional. "The focus is the two leads meeting. The background needs to support that, not distract from it. That rack is a distraction."

We both reached for a loose skein of yarn that had dislodged from a display and rolled across the cutting table, our fingers brushing. I snatched my hand back as if I'd touched a hot stove. Winslow didn't flinch, just replaced the yarn neatly in the stack.

"The quilts are one of the main reasons people come in here." I tried to ignore the lingering warmth where our hands had touched. "They're made by artisans from three counties. They're not background. They're at the heart of the store."

"In the film, the stock of flannel is what's important," he said, as if that explained everything. "The heart of the store, for my purposes, is a particular bolt of red-and-black plaid flannel that Julian will be touching when Callum first sees him."

He spoke about his movie with a kind of passion

that was both ridiculous and, to my intense frustration, a little captivating. His drive to craft perfection was burned in the depths of those critical blue eyes. I almost understood the artistic vision he was describing, before remembering this was my family's legacy he was trying to redecorate.

"We can't just dismantle the store for a single scene," Paige said, her arms crossed.

"I don't want to dismantle it." Winslow gestured around the room with those precise, director's hands. "I want to enhance it. This place has history. I can feel it. I want to capture that. But film is a unique language. A camera needs to be told where to look. Right now, it's a cacophony. I need to create a single, clear note."

Felix looked like he wanted the floor to swallow him whole. "What Landon means," he interjected smoothly, "is that we'd be respectful of all your items. Everything would be carefully moved by our set dressing team and put back as it was."

Winslow moved through the narrow aisle between displays, and I followed, unable to let him out of my sight. As we navigated the tight space, the old floorboards creaked beneath our feet. He stopped so abruptly I nearly collided with him. He stared down, head cocked as if listening to a distant symphony.

Pointing to the floor, he said, "The floorboards. They're perfect. The way they creak... we can use that. Sound up. Callum walks in, the floorboard creaks, Julian looks up from the flannel. It's a moment."

I couldn't help it. I almost smiled. Winslow was so absorbed in his vision, so oblivious to how he was coming across. Not just an arrogant asshole from Hollywood. Landon Winslow was an arrogant, *passionate* asshole from Hollywood. A subtle, but notable, distinction.

I couldn't hold back a comment. "The floorboards have been creaking for decades. They don't need your permission."

A flicker of a smile, sharp and quick, touched his lips. It changed his entire face, softening the harsh lines for a bare instant. And in that instant, another unwelcome jolt went through me.

This was a problem. Winslow was infuriating, dismissive, and treating my home like a play set. And he was also... handsome. Not just generically good-looking, but strikingly so. The intensity that I'd found so irritating pulled me toward him. I wanted to talk about Christmas movies with him. If only he wasn't so... irritating.

I forced myself to be calm, just like I did at a press conference after a losing game. "Look, you can film in here. We signed the contract. But you have to work with us. Some things can't be moved."

"Everything can be moved. It's just a question of logistics."

"Not everything is about logistics. Some things are about respect."

We stared at each other across the cutting table. The air between us hummed with a tension that had nothing to do with quilt racks or floorboards. It was a clash of wills. Of two entirely different ways of seeing the world.

He saw everything as something to be framed, controlled, and perfected. I saw things to be protected, preserved, and honored.

Felix cleared his throat. "Okay! Well! This has been productive. Landon, we have that call with the studio in ten minutes."

Winslow didn't break eye contact with me for several seconds. His sharp jaw was tight. Finally, he gave a curt nod. "Fine. We'll work around the goddamn quilt rack. For now. Send me a revised set plan, Felix. I need to see if I can make the blocking work."

He turned on his heel without another word and strode out of the store. The bell chimed cheerfully in his wake.

Felix shot Paige and me a weary, apologetic

smile. "He's... brilliant," he said, as if that were an excuse for everything. "The best eye in the business. We'll make this place look great. Thank you for your time. We'll be in touch." He scurried out after Winslow.

The store was silent again, the energy from the encounter still crackling in the air.

"Wow," Paige said, her voice flat. "What a charmer."

"He called the lights hideous." I ran a hand through my hair. I was rattled. My pulse raced in a way that it usually only did during a penalty kill.

"He called the quilt rack a distraction. I think I hate him." She paused, eyeing me shrewdly. "You, however... you looked like you were two seconds away from either punching him or kissing him."

My head snapped toward her. "What? No. I definitely wanted to punch him."

"Right." A small, knowing smile, the one that only an older sister could have, played on her lips. She returned to the front counter and reopened her laptop.

"You're not really going to punch anyone, are you?" Rose came up to us.

"No, of course not," I said quickly.

"Good. Even though he was mean about Paw-

paw's quilt rack, momma always says we can't hit people no matter how much they make us mad."

"That's right, and your uncle will follow that advice too." Paige fixed me with a look.

Before I could say anything, the bell chimed again. This time, the faces were friendly, and the stress of Winslow's visit faded.

"There he is! The Pride of Pine Ridge!" Nick Lawson's voice boomed through the store. He was grinning, his arms open for a hug. Behind him, his boyfriend, Shawn Kendrick, followed, an easy smile on his face.

I met Nick halfway for a quick, solid hug. He played for the Boston Blizzard and had been a friend for years. We'd met at a charity event and bonded over comparing pre-game warm-up playlists.

"Great to see you, Nicky." I released him and beckoned his boyfriend into an embrace. "Shawn, it's been too long."

Shawn's warmth was the complete opposite of Landon Winslow's prickly energy. After years of writing hockey romance novels, he'd penned the original screenplay for *Christmas in the Cascades*. It was a huge advancement for his career.

"Aren't they shooting in here?" Nick asked. "I expected more decorations. You know, to match the exterior."

"Oh, it's coming," Paige grumbled, but she was smiling.

Shawn's eyes sparkled with excitement. "You've been here a day now. What do you think? Is it magical? Does it feel like Christmas?"

"It's chaos," I said. "But it's very cool to watch it all happening. Rose gave me a tour yesterday, and I already can't wait to see it all on screen."

I introduced Rose, and Nick and Shawn fawned over her.

"You're a lot nicer than that guy who was just here," she said when Shawn confirmed that he'd come up with the story for the movie.

Shawn's smile faltered. "Ah. You met Landon."

"He wants to throw out Grandpa's quilt rack," Paige interjected.

Shawn winced. "Yeah, that sounds like him. Specific. Visually driven. But he's a genius. I'm not sure how he ended up on this movie, but I was thrilled when I found out. But yeah, his people skills are..."

"Nonexistent?" I supplied.

"A work in progress," Nick finished, putting an arm around Shawn's shoulders. "Come on. Leave the man alone. We just came to see if you wanted to grab a beer at The Keg later."

"Yeah, I'm in." It'd be a welcome escape from

thinking about the fate of the store and the frustrating director. "I could use a beer."

My mind drifted back to the charged standoff with Landon. His complete self-assurance. The deep blue of his eyes. The way he'd looked at me, like I was a puzzle he was trying to solve, or maybe one he wanted to take apart simply to see how it worked.

"Something wrong?" Nick asked, his voice low. He was perceptive. Always had been.

"No. Just... long day."

"Heard that," he said.

Shawn chatted with Paige about a specific yarn he needed for a scarf he was knitting, which was a new hobby he'd picked up for "character research." Nick caught me up on the Pride celebration he and Shawn had attended in Vermont and his stint at the hockey camp Ethan Gallagher ran. I'd go to Ethan's camp in a couple of weeks and looked forward to working with the young players.

Nick and Shawn often stole glances at each other as we talked. Their easy affection was a comfortable, solid thing. They made it work—the distance, the schedules, the separate worlds of writing and hockey. They were proof that a relationship wasn't impossible. I was happy with casual dating, but seeing them sometimes left me wanting more.

A text from Winslow interrupted our catching

up. The director needed to talk to Shawn as soon as possible, so they headed out.

I walked over to the quilt rack and ran my fingers along the smooth oak that my grandfather had shaped. There was a small imperfection in one joint, a place where the glue had seeped out and hardened into a tiny, amber teardrop. I'd asked him once why he'd left that. "Character" was the only answer he ever gave.

I'd told Winslow the rack was the heart of the store. And I'd protect it from developers and directors. No matter how intriguing I found them.

FOUR

Landon

The color-coded schedule on my wall seemed to mock me with its pristine, perfect order. Every block of time was a domino, and a consultant in Vancouver had just knocked over the first one.

My breath hitched. Panic, cold and sharp, jabbed at my ribs. I shoved it down, converting it into one of the few emotions I allowed myself on set: anger.

"What do you mean he's not going to make it?" It took everything I had not to yell at Felix. "Tell his agent I don't care if he has to charter a private jet fueled by the tears of his director. He has a contract and required to be here."

"He's under a force majeure clause, Lan. There's

nothing we can do. He's not coming." Felix's voice came through the phone, thin and tight with the kind of stress he usually reserved for budgetary crises.

I shot to my feet, the limited space of my trailer feeling like a cage. The afternoon sun slanted through the window, casting long rectangles of light across the corkboard where I'd arranged the fourteen-day shoot schedule in a perfect grid of index cards and colored push pins. Tomorrow's card—*Day 3: Hockey Scenes*—glared at me. I grabbed a marker off my desk and added a bright red exclamation point to indicate its critical status.

"That's not an option." I paced—four steps one way, four steps back. The carpet was already showing a faint path where I'd tread this same line several times since we'd started pre-production. "We can't push the hockey scenes. The child actors are a nightmare to reschedule. And, God forbid, if something doesn't go well, we'll need the time to reshoot."

I ran a hand through my hair, mussing it more than it already was. "Pushing this one scene would mean shuffling days' worth of shooting. We'd be rewriting the schedule on the fly, adding overtime we don't have in the budget because we have nothing else ready for that slot."

My voice was rising, laced with a desperation I

despised. "Ted will have my head if we lose even a single shoot day, not to mention two. We can't lose two days, Felix!"

Two days. On a fourteen-day shoot, two days was a death sentence. The studio had allocated two million dollars, which was barely enough to begin with. Every day over schedule would cost additional location fees, cast and crew salaries, equipment rentals.

But the actual cost wasn't financial. It was *Silo*.

If I couldn't deliver this movie on time and on budget, Ted wouldn't be able to come through and fund my project. The deal I'd made—Ted's movie in exchange for mine—would be void.

"I know the stakes," Felix said calmly from the other end of the line. "I'm looking at the same catastrophic domino effect you are."

"Then find another consultant." The weight of impending failure pressed on my chest. "Call the state film commission. Doesn't Seattle have a team? Get me a list of every ex-pro, every college, or high school coach. Every Zamboni driver within a hundred-mile radius. What about our writer's boyfriend?"

There was a pause on the line. A pause that I hated.

"I've already tried all those options. I started with Shawn's boyfriend since he's right here. Unfortunately, Nick has commitments in Seattle for the next few days. Nick, Shawn, and I, however, all agree on our best remaining option." Felix's voice was maddeningly reasonable.

"Who?"

The wait for his reply seemed endless. "Landon..."

"Who, Felix?"

"There is a two-time All-Star, a guy who has been to the Stanley Cup Final, a player known for his high hockey IQ, who is located approximately three hundred yards from our set. And, I'm told, he loves Christmas movies."

The icy knot in my stomach tightened into a block of ice. No. Absolutely not.

"Don't say his name."

"August Reeve," Felix said, completely ignoring me.

"No." The word was sharp and absolute.

"Lan, think about it. It's perfect. The universe has gift-wrapped us a solution."

"The universe has gift-wrapped us an unexploded bomb," I shot back. "He's not a consultant, Felix. He's a star athlete with a small-town hero complex and an attitude problem."

I stopped pacing and stared at the storyboards for "The Awkward Hockey Lesson." The entire scene was based on a delicate balance. It needed to appear real enough to be believable, but cinematic enough to be romantic.

It needed someone I could direct. The objective wasn't to teach Declan how to play hockey, but to teach him how to look like he knew how to play while falling in love.

Chuck Dempsey understood that language. We'd collaborated early in my career on the series of sports commercials, and even then he had good instincts for what worked on film.

August Reeve, with his quiet defiance and his proprietary feelings about his family's damned quilt rack, would not. Whether or not he liked Christmas movies, he'd want it to be real. He'd argue every choice that privileged the shot over the sport. He was the human embodiment of the messy, unpredictable reality I tried so hard to filter out.

And there was something else. Something I didn't want to examine too closely. The memory of his broad shoulders filling the frame of his family's store. The faint scar on his jawline that had inexplicably drawn my eye—a flaw that only made him more magnetic. Equal parts irritating and fascinating.

"He's not on my payroll. He won't take direction.

He'll have opinions." I thought of his brown eyes flashing with that protective fire over everything in the shop. "We already know he has *plenty* of those."

"He has expertise. Authentic expertise. Isn't that what you're always screaming about? Authenticity? You want Declan to look like a real hockey player. Who better to teach him than someone who makes a living doing it? That's why you hired Chuck. It's why you mentioned Nick. And that's why I'm telling you August is our best option for what you're after."

"He thinks I'm an asshole." I dropped into the chair at my desk and rubbed my temples, hoping to ward off the beginnings of a migraine behind my eyes.

"You are an asshole, Lan," Felix said, with the gentle frankness only he was afforded. "You're a brilliant, visionary asshole, but your bedside manner could use some work. This is you making amends. You're asking for his help. It's good politics."

"I don't care about politics. I care about the movie." Of course, the silent, frantic subtext to all of this was *Silo*. This ridiculous holiday romance was the rickety bridge to get to that, and its supports were groaning.

"Are you sure Shawn can't convince his boyfriend to help us?"

"He can't. It's contractual commitments for a

sponsor." Felix paused, then continued with a tone I recognized as the one he used to help keep me calm and centered. "There's no one. No one with any real qualifications who can be here by six a.m. tomorrow. We either ask August Reeve, or we give up the day."

August Reeve triggered memories of Thomas and what I'd had... and lost with him. With August's protective zeal for his family's legacy and his unyielding stance in the store, he was unpredictable. Uncontrollable. Unscriptable.

Thomas, a gallery owner I'd dated for nearly three years, had accused me of scripting our lives like one of my movies. He said I prioritized my shot list over our relationship.

We were in our apartment, his suitcase already packed by the door. Afternoon sunlight streamed through the windows, giving the room just the right ambiance. It was a perfect shot. Romantic devastation in natural light.

"You can't direct people, Landon," he'd yelled, his face flushed with a fury I'd never seen before. "You can't block out our life like it's a scene. Real life is messy. It doesn't hit its marks."

"I'm not trying to direct you." Even as I said it, I realized I was positioning myself for better light, and arranging my face to look sincerely contrite. "I need to finish this script. *Silo* is important, Thomas. It's my shot."

"It's always your shot." His voice became quiet. "Our relationship is just... background action to you. A subplot you service when you have a free moment, but not the A-story. Never the A-story."

He'd picked up his bag and walked out the door, and I'd let him. I'd chosen my art.

I'd buried myself in my work ever since, embracing the control. It was safer. I was better at it.

But Felix had me cornered. The implied threat of having to explain my failure to the studio head was the final checkmate. I leaned my head back against the cool wall of the trailer, staring at the acoustic tile ceiling.

"Fine. You win. I'll ask him." I hated that I had to agree.

"Thanks. I think this could be a good thing."

"It's a necessary thing." I corrected him because I saw nothing good in what was about to happen. "It's triage. Don't mistake it for anything else." I took a breath, bracing myself for the humiliation to come. "Where is he now, do you know?"

"He's meeting up with Shawn and Nick. They told me they were going to see him at The Keg Saloon for a beer."

Of course. A place called The Keg Saloon. It was

perfect. I was going to have to walk into some rustic, wood-paneled watering hole, find the local hero, and beg him to save my movie. It was a scene straight out of one of these schmaltzy films, and I was being forced to play the part of the humbled big-city guy. The irony was suffocating. At the same time though, my mind couldn't help but imagine what that movie might be like.

I grabbed my wallet and keys from the desk. The script for *Silo* sat right next to them, its title page staring back. *Silo. Written and Directed by Landon Winslow.*

The promise felt further away than ever.

I went to the door of the trailer and paused, my hand on the handle. "This is a mistake," I said, mostly to myself.

"It's the only option. Go be charming, Lan. Or, you know, your version of it. Meanwhile, I'll get the basic contract together for him. Same terms we had for Chuck."

I ended the call without replying and shoved the phone in my pocket. I stepped out of the trailer, the oppressive evening heat hitting me. The area was quieter now, with the crew working on some specific decorations for upcoming outdoor scenes.

My chest tightened as I thought about seeing August again. I told myself it was dread. Just dread.

But my quickened pulse made it clear I was lying to myself about that.

I had no choice. I had to go find August Reeve and ask for his help. Inviting the storm onto my set was the only way forward. I could only hope it wouldn't disrupt everything.

FIVE

August

THE KEG SALOON was a Pine Ridge institution—dark wood, worn barstools, and a great jukebox currently playing "Rockin' Around the Christmas Tree." The owners decided to lean into the filming and added some holiday songs, which people actually picked. As someone who has a few festive tunes on my regular playlist, I didn't mind at all.

Nick and Shawn were supposed to meet me here, but they'd texted to say they'd be late. So, I was nursing a beer and trying to map out a strategy to fight Corbin Donovan. All my brain could do, though, was circle back to the futility of it all.

It felt like trying to stop a mudslide with a picket fence. The names I'd typed into my phone's notes app included other business owners who didn't want to sell and a journalist from the county paper. It looked pathetic against Donovan's slick corporate machine.

Then the door swung open, and the energy shifted just like it had in the store.

Winslow stood in the doorway, letting his eyes adjust to the dim light. Taut and angular in his ever-present black, he looked like a predator that had wandered into a petting zoo. Heads turned. Conversations paused. He was a foreign object out of place.

A group of crew from the film sitting at a high top did double-takes, their easy laughs cutting off. I guess the director wasn't someone they expected to see in their off-hours.

His gaze swept the room with the same critical intensity I'd seen in the store. Was The Keg another location?

When his eyes landed on my table, they narrowed. For a second, I thought he might just turn around and leave. His expression was one of profound reluctance.

But he didn't leave. He took a breath, straightened his shoulders, and started walking toward me. He wove through the tables with a tense, deliberate grace. The entire bar seemed to watch the spectacle.

I stayed seated, my hand resting on my beer

bottle. I wasn't going to make this easy for him. Whatever this was, he'd have to come to me.

He stopped at the edge of my table, a neon sign on the wall painted one side of his face in an artificial red light.

"Mr. Reeve." His voice was all business.

"Winslow." I matched his tone and gestured to the empty seat opposite me. "To what do I owe the pleasure?"

He ignored the invitation, choosing to stand—a power move, meant to put me at a disadvantage. It was also a sign of how uncomfortable he was. He wanted this over with as quickly as possible. "I have a business proposition for you."

Taking a deliberately slow sip of beer, I raised an eyebrow. "I'm listening."

"My hockey consultant for the film, Chuck Dempsey, has become unavailable due to a... force majeure event at his previous engagement." He delivered the words like a line from a legal document he'd memorized. "The result is that my production is without the necessary expertise to execute a series of critical scenes scheduled to begin filming tomorrow morning at six."

He was a director through and through. I'd never heard a person talk that way in real life. It was almost charming in its absurdity. Almost.

"So your hockey guy bailed," I translated.

A muscle in his jaw jumped. "The situation is more complex than that, but yes. That is the practical outcome." He shifted his weight, hinting at his discomfort. "Rescheduling the scenes is not a viable option due to talent availability and budgetary constraints. In short, the entire production schedule is in jeopardy."

I studied him. The superior, critical glint in his eyes had vanished, replaced by a barely contained panic. He looked like a man trying to hold a crumbling dam together with nothing but spit and sheer force of will. For all his cool control in the store, this seemed different.

And it gave me a small, satisfying moment of leverage.

"That sounds like a you-problem." I leaned back in the booth.

"It is a me-problem. One which I am proposing to make a you-solution."

"And how do you figure that?"

"You are a professional hockey player." He said it with the enthusiasm of someone reading an autopsy report. "More than qualified to consult on the technical aspects of the scenes in question."

I waited. The silence between us stretched as the

jukebox switched from Christmas cheer to the classic "Landslide."

Winslow let out a quiet, frustrated sigh. "I am offering you the position of hockey consultant on *Christmas in the Cascades*." The words came out in a rush, as if saying them quickly would lessen their impact. "Standard daily rate, plus a consulting credit in the final film. You would report to set tomorrow morning at the Pine Ridge Ice Arena." When I still said nothing, he added, "We need you."

There it was. *We need you*. Three words I'd bet Landon Winslow didn't say often.

"And what exactly would I be consulting on?" I asked, not ready to let him off the hook yet.

His shoulders tensed even further. "We're filming what we call 'The Awkward Hockey Lesson' scene. It's the lead character teaching the other to skate. It's a crucial plot point that establishes their—" he hesitated, looking pained—"romantic chemistry."

I couldn't help the faint smile that tugged at my lips. "So, you need me to make your actors appear like they actually know what they're doing on the ice."

"Essentially, yes." His fingers drummed against his thigh, a small, nervous gesture at odds with his rigid control. "Declan Thorne has never played hockey in his life. The scene requires him to look like a plausible coach, not a Hollywood actor on rental skates. There are also some scenes with some local youth players, and more of Declan."

My gut instinct told me to just say no and watch him squirm. I had enough on my plate. The last thing I needed was to spend time taking orders from this arrogant, prickly man who thought my family's history was a "distraction." Saying no would be easy. It might even be satisfying.

But as I looked at him standing there, his entire production hanging by a thread, another thought surfaced.

I loved Christmas movies.

And here was a chance to peek behind the curtain. He offered me an opportunity to see how it all came together—from the falling fake snow to the crafting of the perfect on-screen romance. The part of me that had watched the *Evergreen* movies so many times I could recite the dialogue was practically vibrating with excitement.

"Felix mentioned you have a... fondness for holiday films," Winslow said carefully, watching my face. "He thought that might be of interest."

I narrowed my eyes. Of course, Shawn would have told that to Felix. "Did he now?"

Then the more practical, more strategic part of my brain kicked in. This job meant being on the inside. I could make sure Pine Ridge wasn't just a caricature of a charming small town. Being part of the crew, I could make sure that they treated my home with the respect it deserved.

It was leverage. It was an opportunity.

The pros were stacking up, heavily outweighing the one major con: the director himself. Dealing with him would be a challenge. Condescending, intense, and distractingly present. The memory of our standoff in the store and that electric charge between us was still fresh. But being a professional athlete meant knowing how to work with difficult people. I'd played with guys far more arrogant than Winslow.

I could handle him.

I hoped.

Grabbing my phone off the table, I opened an email to start a list. "Okay. Let's talk terms."

The relief that flooded Winslow's face was there and gone in a flash. I had him.

"As I said, standard daily consultant rate..." he began.

"I don't want your money," I cut him off. He blinked, surprised. "You'll split my fee between the businesses you're using as locations as well as any that might be affected by business disruptions because of the filming."

He stared at me, his sharp eyes assessing me in a

new light. He clearly hadn't expected that. I could see the gears turning in his head as he re-evaluated.

"That's... acceptable." He finally sat down.

"Good." I continued to type. "Next. My sister, Paige, has final say on anything that gets moved, changed, or touched in our store. Not your producer, not your art department. Her. You have a problem with a quilt rack, you talk to her. And you're polite when you do it."

Annoyance flashed across his face, but he quickly hid it. "Agreed."

"And finally." I looked up from my phone and met his gaze. "You're a guest in this town. Your crew are guests. Act like it. Be respectful of the people and the places here. And remember that this is our home, not just your set."

The challenge hung in the air between us, plain and clear. I was setting the rules. It wasn't only about his hockey scenes. It was about everything.

He held my gaze for a long moment. I expected him to argue, to push back. He was a man used to being in charge. But he gave a single, curt nod.

"We have a deal, Mr. Reeve."

"Call me August. If we're going to be working together, we might as well be on a first-name basis."

"Landon." His voice was still stiff as he extended a hand across the table.

His hand was cool and dry, and his grip firm. The moment our skin touched, a low-level electric current shot up my arm. It was the same charged energy I'd felt in the store, only stronger, amplified by the direct contact. The jolt left me off balance.

It shouldn't have felt like that. Not from him.

His eyes widened slightly, telling me he'd sensed it too. He pulled his hand back a fraction of a second too quick, apparently as caught off guard as I was.

"And I want full access." I grabbed my phone again and added the note. "Not just for the hockey scenes. I want to see how the whole thing works."

Landon's brow furrowed. "You want to... observe the entire production?"

"Is that a problem?" I challenged.

His head tilted slightly as he considered. "No. It's... unusual. But it's acceptable."

The door to the saloon opened, and Nick and Shawn walked in, bringing a gust of warm night air with them. They stopped in their tracks when they saw Landon at my table.

I nodded at them, and Winslow glanced over his shoulder to see who had caught my attention.

"Where should I email this so you can write up our agreement?"

"Let me give you addresses for me and Felix." He reached out, and I handed him my phone.

"Everything okay?" Nick asked as they approached.

Winslow cleared his throat, handed my phone back, and stood up. "Everything's fine. I was just hiring your friend." He turned back to me. "Thank you. I'm glad we came to an agreement. My production assistant will email you the call sheet. Be at the arena at six a.m. Don't be late."

And with that, he turned and walked out of The Keg.

Shawn sat down. "You took the consulting job?"

"I did." My hand still tingled where Landon had touched it.

Nick slid in next to Shawn. "You laid out terms? For a consultant gig on a Christmas movie? Sitting in here?" A slow grin spread across his face. "You're playing hardball with a Hollywood director. Well done."

"He needed me." I echoed Landon's words. "I'm surprised you didn't take the job since it is your boyfriend's film?"

Nick shrugged. "I've got a promotional thing for TruEdge Skates for the next few days, otherwise I would've."

"I admit, despite Winslow's intensity, I am looking forward to watching the movie come together."

"Landon gets stressed about everything," Shawn said. "He's intense. But brilliant. You should see what he did with the town square scenes yesterday. He's going to make Pine Ridge look magical."

"And you're going to help him make hockey look legit," Nick said enthusiastically. "Pro tip: be cautious around Declan if he's got a hockey stick in his hand. I was at the rink a couple of days ago when they did his uniform fitting. He kept moving around the ice like he was trying to play golf with the puck."

I laughed, tension from the encounter with Landon easing. "Noted."

But as Nick and Shawn launched into a story about their time in Maplewood with Ethan during Pride, my mind drifted back to Landon. The way he looked when our hands touched. The feeling that had passed between us.

I was satisfied, though, that I'd gotten what I wanted from our agreement. Plus, I had a front-row seat to how the holiday magic came to life.

SIX

Landon

IT WASN'T EVEN six yet, and the Pine Ridge Ice Arena was already a hive of activity with the entire production nearly set up. Cables snaked under rubber mats. Lights on towering stands bathed the ice as the crew worked to get just the right vibe for the small-town magic we required.

I stood next to the boards, a cup of black coffee warming my hands, and surveyed the scene. The massive Christmas wreaths we'd hung yesterday along the viewing area looked out of place against the industrial gray walls, but they'd be perfect once the cameras rolled.

The Steadicam operator was stretching while the young actors were almost in full gear. Declan sat on a bench, scrolling through his phone, presumably going over his script. The only piece missing was the one I was dreading. August Reeve wasn't here yet, but he would be soon.

I'd spent most of the night staring at my ceiling, replaying my humiliating capitulation at The Keg Saloon. He'd cornered me, negotiated terms like a seasoned agent, and left me feeling like I'd lost even though I'd gotten his services. The memory of his handshake—that startling, static shock—was a sensation that wouldn't fade. The last time I was this unsettled around someone was early in my relationship with Thomas.

"Morning, boss." Felix appeared at my elbow, holding out a tablet with the revised call sheet displayed on the screen. "He's here."

I followed his gaze. August was coming this direction, carrying a hockey bag slung over one shoulder and a pair of worn-looking skates in his hand. He wore a simple gray hoodie and black track pants, the kind of unassuming athletic gear that only emphasized the powerful build beneath. Moving with unhurried confidence, his eyes took in the controlled chaos of the set with calm curiosity. He looked completely at home.

When he saw me, he gave a brief, polite nod. There was no gloating in his expression, no hint of the power he'd wielded last night. He was just a man showing up for a job. He was so damn professional it was irritating.

"Landon," he said as he reached me.

"August," I replied, my tone clipped. "You're on time."

"You said six." He shrugged, as if being punctual was the most obvious thing in the world. He dropped his bag. "Where do you want me?"

I took a sip of my coffee, using the moment to fortify myself. "We're starting with Scene 22, 'The Awkward Hockey Lesson.' Your job is to make Declan Thorne look like he knows how to play and coach hockey. And to make Brandon Atkins look like a believable novice."

August's gaze shifted to Declan, who had abandoned his phone and was attempting to lace his skates with all the dexterity of a man wearing oven mitts. A flicker of—amusement? pity?—crossed August's face.

"Right. Declan. Got it."

He moved his bag out of the way and went over to where Declan sat struggling with his skates. He settled on the bench beside the actor.

"Hi. I'm August." He slipped off his sneakers and set them aside. "Need a hand with those?"

"Oh my God, yes. These laces don't seem to be

long enough." Declan's face relaxed. "And I'm Declan." They fist bumped. "It's good to meet you. I hope you can get me to do what Landon wants."

"We'll make it work." August's smile was calm. "Let's get you laced up."

I watched, transfixed, as August pulled a funny-looking tool from one of his skates. It was a bent metal rod with a hook on one end and a triangle handle on the other. Neither of them was talking loud enough for me to hear, but Declan paid attention as August put his skates on and laced up, using the tool to work the laces. There was a patient steadiness to his instruction as Declan tried to do it. Brandon also joined them to get his skates on.

Once that was done, the trio went out to the center of the ice, and the difference was stark. August moved with ease, his blades making a soft hissing sound against the pristine surface. Declan and Brandon were a different story, with Brandon only being a little steadier than his co-star. August immediately worked to get them stabilized.

I felt a twinge of gratitude. Perhaps this consultation wouldn't be the disaster I'd feared.

After they'd had a few minutes on the ice, it was time to get going. "Alright, positions, everyone!" I slipped into director mode. "Declan, Brandon, let's block this through."

August skated over to the rink entrance where a group of five child actors in hockey gear were fidgeting under the watchful eye of a production assistant. The kids would be in a later scene, where Declan's character coaches youth hockey, but they were here early for wardrobe and blocking.

"Hey, guys." August's voice was warm in a way he didn't use with me. "Excited about your big movie moment?"

The children's reactions were instantaneous.

"You're August Reeve," one boy exclaimed. "I saw you play in Seattle last season! You scored the winning goal."

August smiled a smile that transformed his face as he crouched down to the kids' eye level. "I think we need to be quiet so they can work. But tell you what, if you listen to the crew and do a great job today, maybe we can all scrimmage later. Sound good?"

The children nodded enthusiastically, their earlier restlessness gone. With a few words, he'd turned a potential headache into a group ready to do what they were told. It was the kind of situation I normally had to micromanage. He'd done it as if it were nothing.

The first scene to shoot was simple in concept. Callum, the hockey player, tries to teach Julian, the architect, how to skate. There's some witty banter, some physical comedy, and it culminates in Julian stumbling into Callum's arms for a charged, almost-kiss moment.

It was pure romance-trope catnip. It also required a level of physical grace that Declan Thorne didn't possess.

"Okay, Declan, you're showing him the basics," I instructed from my position at the monitors. "Demonstrate a glide. Keep it simple. Brandon, you're trying to copy him, but you're tense, unsure. All your control from your big-city life is gone here. You're vulnerable."

Declan pushed off, his movements stiff and overly deliberate. He looked less like a hockey star and more like a robot learning to walk on ice. Brandon, for his part, shuffled forward, windmilling his arms in a caricature of being off balance.

I squeezed my eyes shut for a second. "Cut. No. Declan, it's too staged. It needs to be effortless. Brandon, less flailing. You're a sophisticated architect, not a cartoon character."

"He has to bend his knees." August's voice came from beside me. I hadn't even realized he'd glided over. He stood against the boards, his arms crossed over his chest. His proximity was... distracting.

"I'm directing here."

"And I'm consulting." He cocked an eyebrow as he looked at me. "Declan's all in his upper body. The power comes from his legs. He has to get his center of gravity down. Give me a second."

August skated out and talked Declan through it again. I didn't understand how he could keep so calm since he was repeating himself. He put his hands on Declan and moved him like an action figure, nearly putting him in a sitting position.

It didn't take long for Declan to try it again, bending his knees, sinking into a skater's crouch. He pushed off again. The difference was immediate and startling. The movement was smoother, more power-ful. He looked like a person who had been on skates before. While Declan practiced, August moved over to Brandon and coached him through how to be more convincingly tentative.

Felix caught my eye from across the ice and gave me a subtle, smug nod. I ignored him.

"Okay, better," I conceded grudgingly. "Now, the dialogue. Brandon, you have the line about the ice being 'deceptively slippery.' Let's have that as you start to wobble."

We worked through the first part of the scene for the next hour. It became a strange three-way dialogue. I'd give direction based on the emotional arc of the scene, Declan and Brandon would try to execute it, and August would interject practical corrections that invariably made it better.

"I need you to grab his arm for support, Brandon," I said.

"He wouldn't grab his arm." August spoke so only I'd hear him. "He'd more likely end up grabbing his jersey. Your costume department might hate me, but it'll look real."

"The jersey grab isn't romantic."

"It's real. And it forces them closer together. Brandon has to bunch the fabric to get a good grip, which brings his hand right up against Declan's chest. If anything, it's more intimate than an arm grab."

I opened my mouth to argue, then closed it as I visualized the shot. He was right. It was a better angle, a more organic interaction. "Fine," I said to August before turning back toward the actors. "Brandon, grab the jersey."

We went back and forth like that on a dozen different details. The angle of a hockey stick. The way someone would fall. The proper way to get back up. The distance between them during instruction.

Our arguments were short, sharp, and surprisingly efficient. August wasn't just being contradictory for the sake of it. Every note he gave was rooted in an unassailable logic I couldn't deny.

He was making my movie better.

And I hated him for it.

But I also found the rapid-fire exchange of ideas, the clash of our two different kinds of expertise, to be exhilarating. It was like a high-speed chess match. Each of his suggestions forced me to recalibrate to manage both the technical reality and the emotional story I was trying to tell.

It reminded me of the early days with Thomas, when we'd spend hours discussing shots I wanted to try, the framing of a particular scene. The difference was that Thomas eventually tired of the back-and-forth. August showed no signs of backing down. He delivered every challenge with the same calm certainty.

The crew watched, amused. I caught the smiles they were trying to hide. They saw the friction, but they probably also saw the chemistry crackling between us. Professional chemistry, I told myself. That's all it was.

During a break, Declan approached August, a nervous grin on his face.

"Hey, man," Declan said, awkwardly shifting his weight on his skates. "Would it be okay if I got a selfie? I'd like to post about the guy helping me turn into a hockey player."

August smiled. "Of course." He posed with

Declan, their heads together as Declan held the phone in front of him. "Your crossovers are getting better, by the way. Just remember to push all the way through."

"Thanks." Declan beamed under the praise. "For everything. This would be... I don't even want to think about what it might be."

The interaction left me with an odd, uncomfortable sensation in my chest. August made it look so easy. The way he connected with people—the kids, Declan, Brandon, the grips who asked him about the Mountaineers' chances next season. It was effortless.

It was the opposite of how I operated. I directed every interaction, planned every response. Even with Thomas, I'd always been trying to frame the perfect moment. "You're not directing me, Landon," he'd said once after I'd tried to orchestrate a romantic dinner. "I'm not one of your actors. I'm supposed to be your boyfriend."

This wasn't the time for memories, so I shoved them aside. "Okay. Let's move to the stumble. The almost-kiss. This is the centerpiece of the scene. It needs to be perfect." I carefully made my way across the ice to the actors. "Brandon, you're getting more confident. You glide on your own, get a little speed, and then you lose it. You're going to fall forward, and Declan, you catch him. Your faces should be inches apart. We hold on that moment of shock, attraction. Got it?"

They nodded.

I retreated to the monitors. "Action!"

Brandon pushed off, a little too fast, a little too wobbly. It was believable. But as he "lost it," he pitched forward in a way that was unnatural, his arms pinwheeling. Declan caught him in a stiff, awkward embrace.

"Cut!" I groaned. "It's clunky. There's no grace."

"That's not going to work," August said quietly. "I didn't realize you were going to do it like that."

I shot him a glare. "He's got to be able to fall forward."

"You don't fall forward like that. Your feet go out from under you. You fall backward or to the side."

"I need him to fall into Declan's arms. It's a romance."

August looked at the actors, and the piercing stare was mesmerizing. After a moment, he nodded. "You've got Brandon in figure skating skates, so he can catch the toe pick. The skate stops dead, but his body keeps going. It's sudden, it's a real thing that happens, and it will throw him forward." He paused. "Give me a few minutes to show them."

Before I could object, he skated out to the actors.

"Declan, stand here," he commanded. "Be ready. Okay?"

Declan nodded and partially outstretched his arms.

August skated away, then turned and came back toward him at a controlled speed. "So, Brandon tries to stop," he narrated, his voice smooth and clear, "but he's a novice, so he does it wrong. He tries to dig in with his toe."

Even though August wore hockey skates, he faked the toe pick perfectly. He came to a near-instant halt, and his body, propelled by momentum, pitched forward. He fell into Declan's waiting arms, his face inches from the actor's. The movement was realistic, surprising, and a thousand times more effective than the clumsy stumble I'd imagined.

He held the pose for a beat, his brown eyes looking up at Declan. The entire set was silent. In that moment, he wasn't a consultant or an athlete. He was a performer creating the cinematic moment I needed.

Then he straightened up and looked over at me. "Like that."

I stared at him, my mind blank for a second. The director in me was thrilled. The man who had bet his entire career on controlling every variable was floored. August had solved my problem with a grace and intelligence I hadn't anticipated. Being so thoroughly outmaneuvered and one-upped should have been infuriating. Instead, a hot, unwelcome current of attraction rolled through me.

It was the same feeling I'd had when I first met Thomas at an art gallery opening. He'd been explaining the light techniques in a stark black-and-white photograph, and his insight had caught me off guard. The way he saw what I'd missed drew me in.

Working with August had that same sense of being challenged and pushed to see differently. But it was more visceral. August made me feel physically off balance, just like Brandon and Declan had been before he'd coached them.

"Right." I cleared my throat. "Yes. Like that. Good. That's good." I turned to my actors, desperate to break the spell. "You saw that? Do that."

We ran the scene again with August's adjustments. It worked. It was perfect. Brandon's stumble was surprising and real, and Declan's catch was solid and protective. When their faces were inches apart, there was a genuine spark of shock and chemistry.

I watched through the monitor, completely absorbed. "Hold it... hold it..." I murmured, encouraging them to keep looking at each other. And then, "Cut! Perfect! Print that! Moving on!"

A wave of relief and satisfaction washed over the set, and the crew started resetting for the next shot.

August came back over to me. "See?" A small, infuriatingly smug smile played on his lips. "Authenticity can be romantic."

"Don't get cocky," I said, but there was no heat in it. "You solved one problem."

"It was the biggest one you had." His eyes glinted with amusement.

He was right, and we both knew it.

I owed him. More than that, I respected him.

It was a disconcerting feeling. Respect was something I reserved for a very select group of cinematographers and editors. It was not something I was supposed to feel for a stubborn, small-town hockey player who had taken advantage of me needing him to work for me.

"Maybe." It was the closest thing to a thank you I could manage. "But we've still got the youth hockey sequence to shoot."

"The kids will be great," he said, confident. "They're excited to be part of it."

I smiled despite myself. "Funny, they weren't excited when my AD was trying to wrangle them this morning."

August shrugged. "Kids know when you're

trying too hard to control them. You have to meet them where they are."

The simple statement hit harder than it should have.

Meet them where they are.

Not direct them. Not control them. It was another approach opposite to how I navigated the world.

The rest of the morning went smoothly. August's presence had a calming effect on the set. He gave quiet notes, demonstrated drills for both the child actors and Declan. His competent authority made my job easier.

Our earlier friction had settled into a kind of energetic rhythm. A rapid-fire debate over blocking would end with him conceding a point with a wry grin. A disagreement about a line reading full of hockey jargon ended the moment he acted it out himself, showing a surprising nuance that made the dialogue click into place.

By the time we wrapped the rink scenes an hour ahead of schedule, I didn't know what to do with myself. The day had not been the disaster I'd antici-pated. It had been a success. A success largely due to August Reeve.

As the crew packed up, I reviewed the playback on my portable monitor, checking the takes one last time, even before dailies. The shots were good. Better than good. The hockey lesson had a realism that elevated it beyond holiday-movie schmaltz.

August's small suggestions had added layers of texture and authenticity that I wouldn't have captured on my own. I'm not sure Chuck Dempsey would've gotten the same results if he'd been here.

My focus should have been on the actors, on the light, on framing the shot. But as I watched the scene of the almost-kiss, my eyes kept drifting to the edge of the monitor, where August was visible in the background for a split second before he stepped out of the shot. He just stood there, watching. He looked like he belonged there.

I hit pause, the image of Declan and Brandon frozen in their embrace. But it was August I saw in my mind's eye. The way he moved on the ice, the focus in his eyes, the confidence that was so different from my own coiled intensity. My deal with him was supposed to be a simple transaction. A temporary fix. But watching him today, working with him, arguing with him, I realized it was nothing of the sort.

One of the grips said something that got August laughing. It pulled my attention from the monitor. I didn't catch the words, but August's reaction was unguarded. The laughter softened his features and erased the formality we'd maintained. Several crew members joined in, and I watched as August clapped the grip on the shoulder, saying something that made the man beam with pride.

This was going to be a problem.

A much, much bigger problem than a delayed hockey consultant or a stubborn quilt rack.

This problem stood twenty feet away, connecting with my crew, looking perfectly comfortable. And I had the terrifying feeling that I'd regret giving him full access to the set for the rest of the shoot.

SEVEN

August

AFTER THE SUCCESS at the rink, the tension between me and Landon Winslow changed. It was still there, a low hum beneath the surface, but it was no longer purely antagonistic.

I leaned against the side of a lighting cart as Landon directed a scene in the town square. Yesterday's work at the ice rink had left me thinking about the director a lot. When my solution for the almost-kiss had worked, the look of genuine respect in his eyes took me by surprise.

It reminded me of my first year with the Mountaineers, when Coach Brennan had pulled me aside after a brutal practice. "You're not just muscle, Reeve," he'd said, squeezing my shoulder. "You've got vision. You see the play that could come together. Don't let anyone tell you different. Or try to take that away from you."

I hadn't expected to find that same recognition in Landon's sharp blue gaze.

He wasn't the Hollywood hack I'd pegged him for. Beneath all of his controlling bluster was someone who cared about his craft. Who could admit when someone else had a better idea.

"See what I mean?" Shawn's voice came from beside me. He'd wandered over from where he'd been watching the monitor with Landon and offered me a bottle of water he'd snagged from somewhere. "He's kind of brilliant."

"He's... intense," I said, taking a sip of the cool liquid.

"That man sees the world differently than the rest of us." Shawn kept his focus on Landon. "He sees it in frames, in cuts, in moments."

Landon crouched and spoke in low tones to the actress playing the town baker. She nodded, her expression softening. When he called "action," she handed Declan a gingerbread cookie with a maternal warmth that hadn't been there before.

My chest felt tight. I understood that kind of focus, a single-minded drive to perfect a craft until it became second nature. I had it on the ice. But I'd always kept it contained to the rink. Landon Winslow lived in that space of absolute intensity.

I found it intimidating... and magnetic.

The shot wrapped, and Landon called for a thirty-minute lunch break. The carefully constructed magic of the scene dissolved into the mundane reality of a film set. Cast and crew headed for the catering tent.

Except Declan, who had responded to a small cluster of people behind barricades calling his name. Many of them had their phones out. I hadn't paid attention to them before, but now as he posed for selfies, I noticed how large the crowd was.

"I don't think those are locals."

He spent time with each person who wanted a picture.

"Yeah, seems like the word is getting out. Mrs. Miller told me this morning that her sales have jumped over the past couple of days." Shawn pulled out his phone, scrolling quickly before showing me the screen. "Declan and Brandon have both been posting behind-the-scenes stuff. Millions of followers between them. People are making trips to come watch."

I glanced back at the small crowd. A few were drifting away, likely looking for somewhere to eat.

Hopefully, this tiny economic ripple helps some of the business owners struggle less.

"Do you think I can post some of the pics I shot yesterday?" Maybe some of my images could help, even though they were indoors.

"Probably. You should talk to the publicist to make sure. There are some rules around what they want posted. No spoilers, and such. I can send her your way?"

"That'd be great. I'm headed to the deli. Can I get you anything?"

"I'm good. I need to head back to the room and get some writing done so I hit the deadline for the next book."

"Alright, catch you later."

The afternoon sun was relentless as I walked down Main Street. The energy of the film set faded, replaced by the normal rhythm of Pine Ridge. Tourists shopping. Locals saying hello as I passed. It was a relief to be away from the hum of generators and the strange pull of a certain director.

"August Reeve. Just the man I needed to find."

I stopped, my shoulders tensing before I even turned around. I knew that voice. It belonged to a well-dressed wrecking ball.

Corbin Donovan leaned against the brick wall of the hardware store in a gray suit. He was smiling, but his gaze was cold and assessing, like a shark sizing up a meal. I had no idea how he wasn't sweating in the heat.

"Donovan. I don't have time right now." I took off walking again.

"This will only take a moment." He fell into step beside me. I didn't want to walk with him, but on the narrow sidewalk, I had little choice. "I saw you on set this morning. Quite the local hero, aren't you? Hockey star, movie consultant. Is there anything you can't do?"

The condescension was so thick I could have cut it with a knife.

"Just helping where I can."

"Of course you are. Pine Ridge's favorite son, always looking out for the little guy." He gestured at the storefronts we were passing. "Which is why I'm sure you'll come to see that my proposal is what's best for this town. It's about progress, August. It's about bringing this place into the twenty-first century."

My hands clenched into fists in my pockets. "This town has a history, Donovan. It has a soul. It doesn't need to be in the twenty-first century, and you can't put a price on it."

"Oh, but you can," he said with a chilling certainty. "I've run the numbers. A luxury lodge with artisan shops, a high-end spa... we'd create a destination. Jobs will triple. Property values will skyrocket. Your family's shop, for example. The offer I made is four times the property's current assessed value."

We'd stopped in front of Miller's Bakery. Through the window, I saw Mrs. Miller waiting on the lunch crowd—and today it was a crowd. Mr. Henderson from the hardware store was coming out of the bakery, a coffee in his hand. He nodded at me, his expression tightening when he saw who I was with.

"Like I said, our place isn't for sale." My voice dropped to something of a low growl. "None of this is."

"That's not entirely true." Donovan's voice carried just enough for the passersby to hear. "I've had productive conversations with several of your neighbors. The Millers are considering. So are the Patels at the market."

My stomach dropped. I knew things were tight for everyone, but hearing him name names made it real in a way it hadn't been before.

"It's only because you're dangling money in front of people who are struggling." I was aware of the small audience we were attracting. Two visitors with shopping bags had stopped to watch, and capture the interaction on their phones. Mrs. Thompson from the post office was hovering nearby. "But what happens when your luxury development fails? When the tourists stop coming? These businesses have sustained this town for generations."

"Generations of decline. My project breaks ground in six months. The first phase will be completed within a year. The property tax revenue alone will allow the town to do so much. Progress is coming, August. The only question is whether you'll be part of it, or a roadblock to be removed."

The casual threat in his words sent a hot jolt of anger through me. He was driving a wedge through town. I took a step closer, invading his space. He didn't back up, but I saw a flicker of wariness in his eyes.

"You call this progress? Tearing down a hundred years of history to build another soulless resort for rich people from the city?" I was barely controlling my volume now. "This isn't progress. It's greed."

Mrs. Miller had come to the door of the bakery. She was watching us, her expression conflicted. I saw the calculation in her eyes. The weight of bills. Donovan offered a way out.

"The reality, August, is that your emotional attachment is clouding your judgment." Donovan's voice dropped to a confidential tone that was somehow more insulting than if he'd shouted. "You come back here, what, a few weeks a year? You play hockey in Colorado. You have a life beyond this little town. But you're signing these people's death warrants out of sentimentality."

His words hit like a check into the boards. It was my deepest fear voiced aloud—that I was the outsider. That my NHL career had somehow disqualified me from fighting for my hometown.

"I've made my final offer to your sister. She can retire. You can focus on hockey instead of propping up a failing business. It's the smart play, August."

My vision tunneled, a red haze creeping at the edges. For a split second, my muscles tensed, and I felt the energy jolt that comes before a brawl on the ice.

"Get the hell out of my town." I hated that I couldn't keep my voice from shaking with rage. "You and your bullshit revitalization project. We don't want it. We'll fight you."

Donovan's smug expression didn't waver. He simply straightened his tie, unruffled. "Fight me with what? A petition? A bake sale? This is business, not one of your feel-good movies. The town council is beginning to see the considerable benefits of my plan. It's a matter of when, August, not if. Take the offer. It's the smartest play you have left."

He clapped me on the shoulder, a gesture of false camaraderie that felt like a slap. Then he turned and walked away, disappearing into the crowd, leaving me standing on the sidewalk, trembling with useless anger.

He'd played me perfectly, goading me into a public outburst while he remained calm and reasonable.

To anyone watching, I was the hothead. He was the voice of progress. No doubt the tourists already had it up on social media. Not the message that would bring more visitors to town.

I leaned against the brick wall of the bakery, pressing the palms of my hands into my eyes, trying to calm down. The fight seemed impossible. He had money and influence beyond what I had.

Mrs. Miller approached, her kind expression creased with worry. "Augie, don't let him get to you. He's just... he's persuasive, that's all."

"Are you really thinking of selling?" I asked, not wanting to know the answer.

She looked away. "Frank's knees are getting worse. The doctor says he needs surgery. And with the bank breathing down our necks... We haven't decided yet."

I nodded, unable to find any words that wouldn't

sound like hollow reassurance. She squeezed my arm and went back inside.

The weight of it all—the store, the town, my family's legacy—felt as if it was going to crush me. I just stood there, inhaling the scent of baked goods, as defeat settled over me.

For a long moment, I stayed like that, waiting for the shaking in my hands to stop. When it finally did, I pushed off the wall and started toward the park.

All I needed was a minute to myself.

I made a beeline for my favorite bench under a tree at the edge of the pond. This place was special. It's where I'd learned to skate the winter I was four, while Dad watched from here as I played with my friends.

I'd barely sat down when I heard a crunch of the gravel path behind me. Every muscle tensed, ready for another round with Donovan, or maybe one of the business owners who planned to sell and wanted me to stop making waves.

Instead, a familiar lean figure came into view, a half-eaten apple in his hand. The sight of him made me freeze. His usual black t-shirt was wrinkled, and a thin film of sweat covered his forehead from the day's heat.

Had he seen the confrontation?

A fresh wave of humiliation washed over me.

The last thing I wanted was for him to see me lose my cool like that.

"That looked intense." His voice was unusually subdued as he answered my question.

"It was nothing." I ran both hands through my hair, wishing the bench would swallow me.

He didn't reply. He just took a bite of his apple, the crunch loud. I expected him to make a sarcastic comment. Or, hopefully, he'd turn and walk away.

But he stood there. Waiting.

The silence stretched, and it was more unnerving than any question he could have asked. Against my better judgment, I talked.

"He's a developer. Wants to buy up Main Street, tear it all down, and build some glass-and-steel monstrosity he calls a luxury lodge."

"I met him the other day. Donovan." Landon took another bite.

"That's him." I kicked at the ground in front of me. "He thinks because he's got money, he can just roll in here and gut this place, and we're all supposed to thank him for it." I let out a humorless laugh. "And the worst part is, he might be right."

I finally looked up at him. I was prepared for a look of pity or disinterest. But his expression was one of quiet focus. That intense gaze that he usually reserved for a shot fixed on me. He wasn't looking at

me as if I were a problem or a project. He was just...
looking.

The unexpected quality of his attention spurred me to say more.

"He said the town council's on his side. He's got some of the other business owners convinced. Says I'm selfish for trying to stand in the way of progress."

Landon finished his apple, tossing the core into a nearby trashcan with a precise flick of his wrist. He wiped his hands on his black jeans. My pulse sped up as I thought about what those hands could do to me.

I shut the thought down before it went any further. I couldn't think that. Not now. Not ever.

"He's an asshole," Landon said.

It was so direct, so blunt, that it startled a laugh out of me. A real one this time. "Yeah." A small piece of my tension dissipated. "Yeah, he is."

"What's your family's store worth to him?" It wasn't an idle question. It was direct. The same way he'd ask questions on set.

"Financially? Three million according to his latest offer. More than it's worth on paper." I shifted, making space on the bench for him. "Strategically? Everything. We're in the middle of the block, so he can't get the whole thing without us. And we own it outright, both the land and the building."

Landon nodded and took a seat next to me. His expression was thoughtful. "So you're the lynchpin."

"I guess. There are other holdouts too, but we might be the biggest."

My gaze focused on the shadow of stubble along his jaw. I hadn't noticed it before. It softened him, made him look less like the sharp-edged director and... more like someone I wanted to know off set. I shoved that idea aside too.

We sat for another moment.

He didn't offer to start a viral marketing campaign. He didn't suggest I call a high-powered lawyer he knew in LA. He didn't try to script a solution. He just sat there and let me be.

I got to be angry and defeated and unsure, and he didn't try to fix a single damn thing.

The weight on my shoulders didn't disappear, but it shifted. It was the strangest thing. This man who had come into my life and tried to change everything about my family's store was the only one who didn't seem to want to change me and my need to fix this problem.

Two ducks flew in and landed on the lake, and I focused on them. "When I was a kid, I'd sleep in the store sometimes. My dad would set up a sleeping bag in the back room. He'd tell me I was guarding the place, that I was its protector." My gaze shifted toward Landon. "I guess I still think that's my job."

That memory was something I'd never shared with Paige, though it's one I keep coming back to. There's so much wrapped up in the store for me, even though I'm not here taking care of it full time.

"It's a lot to carry." His voice remained neutral.

I looked at him, really looked at him. In the shade of the tree, his blue eyes were darker, more like deep water than clear sky. A strange flutter moved through my chest as I also caught the light dusting of hair visible at the V-neck of his t-shirt.

His walkie-talkie broke the spell as it beeped twice, coming to life. "Landon? We're ready with the next setup."

Landon stayed still. "You going to be okay?"

I held his gaze, those eyes that I found more intriguing than I should.

"Yeah." I meant it too. I'd thought I wanted to be alone, but it turned out what I needed was to be around the right person. "I'll be fine."

He gave a single nod, stood, and headed back to the set.

Our hands never touched. Our bodies never made contact. But something had happened on this bench. He'd seen me at my lowest, and instead of trying to prop me up, he had simply sat with me.

After a few minutes, I headed back to Main Street, feeling settled again.

As Mrs. Thompson, one of the clerks at the post office, approached, she smiled. "You know, Augie, that Donovan fellow's got a slick way about him, but he doesn't know Pine Ridge. We're tougher than we look."

"Yeah." I returned her smile. "We are."

As she passed me, I turned toward the film set. Landon was talking to Declan and Brandon, and I felt the pull between us. I wanted to join him and hear what he was saying. To be around his energy. And to be near the Christmas magic he was creating, because in that world, the store and the town would be saved.

If only this were a real Christmas movie where I could get the guy and save the town.

EIGHT

Landon

Main Street was quiet except for the hum of our generators and the hushed voices of my crew as they transformed the century-old Reeve's Textiles into something both real and magical. Production lights mixed with the morning sun to cast long shadows through the front windows, where my set decorators were putting the finishing touches on holiday garlands and twinkling string lights.

I'd been here since 4:30, overseeing every detail. The Christmas-in-July transformation was festive without being garish. Wreaths hung from wooden beams. Ribbon wound around display cases. I'd gone with the art director's suggestion to use the store's actual merchandise rather than props—bolts of red and green flannel, spools of metallic thread, the arti-sanal works from locals.

My stomach twisted with an anxiety I wasn't used to. Yesterday at the park, August had been so raw, so vulnerable. The memory of his frustrated hurt after confronting Donovan had stayed with me all night. I'd heard the deep attachment he had to this store, to this town.

I wanted to get this right. Not just for my movie, but for him.

"What's the final decision on the quilt rack?" One of the set decorators asked.

"It stays where it is." I didn't even have to think about it. "It's a focal point now, not an obstacle."

She nodded, surprised but pleased.

The bell above the door jingled, and August and Paige entered. They stopped just inside, taking in the transformation. Paige's expression was guarded, her arms folded across her chest. But August's eyes widened, scanning the space with a mixture of wari-ness and something I'd swear was wonder.

"Morning." I hoped my voice didn't give away the anxiety I felt about August seeing the space.

"Wow." He drew out the word as his gaze moved from the twinkling lights to the wreaths to the care-fully arranged displays. "It's like the store got swal-lowed by Santa's workshop but in the best way."

I watched his face, searching for signs of disapproval. "We tried to respect the original layout. Your grandfather's quilt rack is still there. We just highlighted it with some cedar boughs."

Paige walked to the rack, running her fingers along the wood. "You moved the alpaca display." Her voice held more observation than accusation.

"Just temporarily." I gestured to where we'd relocated it. "It's all documented to go back exactly as it was."

August moved deeper into the store. He stopped at a newly arranged display of flannel, where we'd highlighted the particular bolt of red-and-black plaid mentioned in the script.

"This is what they're fighting over in the scene?" He touched the fabric, letting it slide between his fingers.

"Yes, Julian will be examining it when Callum first sees him."

Picking up the bolt, he smiled. "Paige, do you remember that Dad used to have a shirt in this exact pattern?"

The comment shouldn't have affected me, but it did. His connection to this place seemed woven into its physical fabric. The realization made my chest tighten.

Paige went to stand with August and laughed as

she touched the flannel. "Oh, my God. Mom hated that shirt, but he loved it because it was so soft. This feels like it too."

"Right?" August's eyes got a mischievous glint that sent a jolt of excitement through me. "We should totally send them some of this." He looked at me. "What happens to this once the shoot is finished?"

I was dumfounded. I hadn't expected any of this. "Um. It shows up again in a couple of other shots we haven't done yet. Plus, some of it will be used to create additional props. But I imagine we won't use it all."

"Well, I'd like to buy whatever's left." He went back to Paige. "Maybe I'll subtly work some of this into a project for them."

Work it into a project? What did that mean? I had questions, but this wasn't the time.

Felix appeared at my side with a tablet that was already showing camera feeds. I was thankful so I could focus on something else. "We're ready for the blocking rehearsal. Brandon and Declan are in hair and makeup and will be here in the next few minutes."

I nodded but turned back to the siblings. "Does everything meet with your approval?" I hated how tentative I sounded. Since when did I care what anyone outside of the art director and DP thought about the set design?

August looked around again, his brown eyes reflecting the twinkling lights. "It's strange, especially in the summer, but nice. Like seeing your house through someone else's eyes."

I nodded, understanding what he meant.

"You did good," Paige said. "It's our store, but elevated. And honestly, some of these decorating ideas might be recreated come November." Out of the corner of my eye, I caught the art director smiling.

"Good." I took a last look around the transformed space. It was time to get this going. "Alright. Stand-ins in position, please."

Two production assistants stood in for our actors while I worked out the camera movements with my DP. We were planning a complex tracking shot that would follow Julian as he moved through the shop, eventually bringing him face-to-face with Callum at the flannel display.

"Something's wrong." I stepped back from the monitor and framed the shot with my hands.

Felix gave me a questioning look.

"The background. It's too staged." I gestured toward the empty counter, where someone should be working.

A solution presented itself, sudden and obvious. I turned to where August and Paige were watching from the side.

"You should both be in the scene."

Paige blinked. "Excuse me?"

"As background. Behind the counter. Doing what you normally do. Like the day we were here to check out the space, you were both there."

August's eyebrows rose. "You want us to be extras?"

"Yes." I moved toward them, energized by the idea. "But you're not performing. You're just... being. The store isn't just a backdrop. It's a character in this scene. And you're part of it."

"I'm not an actress," Paige said flatly.

"You don't have to act. Just do what you'd do if we weren't here. The camera will barely focus on you, but your presence will help make the store real for the viewer."

August studied me with his perceptive eyes. I saw the wheels turning. "So we'd just be working. While your actors do the scene."

"Exactly."

"And we'd be in the movie?" A hint of excitement crept into his voice.

"Technically, yes." I couldn't help but smile at

his barely concealed interest. "Background only. You won't have lines."

Paige looked skeptical, but August nudged her. "Come on, Paigey. How often do you get to be in a Christmas movie?"

She rolled her eyes, but her resistance crumbled. "Fine. But I'm not wearing a costume. And if I look ridiculous on screen, that's on you." She jabbed a finger into August's chest.

"You won't look ridiculous," I said as August chuckled at his sister.

An hour later, we were ready for the first take. Brandon as Julian and Declan as Callum were in position. The gimbal operator was set after running through the tracking shot a couple of times. August and Paige stood behind the counter, August showing Paige something on his phone while she arranged a display of holiday ribbon.

"Quiet on set!" The AD called.

I moved to my monitor, hyper-focused yet aware of August watching me from the counter.

"And... action!"

Brandon entered through the front door, the bell jingling above him. He moved through the store with the precise choreography we'd rehearsed, his expression shifting from curious to enchanted as he took in the Christmas wonderland. The camera tracked with him as he approached the flannel display.

On cue, Declan emerged from behind a shelf, carrying a stack of fabric. Their eyes met over the red-and-black plaid bolt. The chemistry was immediate and exactly what the meet-cute needed.

"I wouldn't have pegged you for a flannel guy," Declan said, delivering his line with just the right mix of charm and hesitation.

Brandon's response was exactly right, the slight New England accent we'd developed for his character coming through. "I'm not. Usually. But there's something about this one."

Behind them, August and Paige moved naturally in the background, their presence adding just what the scene needed.

"Cut! Perfect!" I couldn't contain my satisfaction. "Let's go again from the top. Same energy."

We shot the scene four more times, so we had some variations and close-ups. Between takes, I glanced at August, gauging his reaction. He was fully engaged, watching the process with an intensity that matched my own. Once, when I called for an adjustment to the lighting, our eyes met across the store. He gave me a small nod that felt like approval.

"You're different today," he said during a brief break while we reset. "More... relaxed."

The comment caught me off guard. "Am I?"

"I think so." His eyes held mine a beat too long. "You've still got the precision for your vision, but you haven't snapped or yelled once."

I recognized the parallel to how I'd felt watching him on the ice. We were both fluent in our own worlds, and somehow, those worlds were starting to overlap.

As planned, by lunchtime, we'd captured all the angles we needed. The crew began packing up equipment, and resetting the store so it looked like we were never there.

"I need to go." Paige checked her watch. "I teach a weaving class at the community center at 12:30."

"Thank you for your help," I said, meaning it more than she probably realized.

After she left, the store emptied quickly as most of the crew went to lunch before the next location. Soon, only a skeleton team remained. Felix coordinated the load out, and the few production assistants getting the remaining items packed.

August stood by the counter, watching as the Christmas transformation was being dismantled, leaving a strange hybrid of holiday cheer and the everyday look of the store.

"Want to see what we shot?" I approached him with a tablet in hand.

He looked surprised but nodded excitedly.

I joined him, and we stood close together, shoulders nearly touching, as I cued up the footage.

On the small screen, Reeve's Textiles sparkled. The warm lighting caught the gleam of polished wood and the cheer of holiday decorations. The camera moved smoothly through the space, capturing every aspect of the store.

"That's how you see it?" he asked.

I glanced at him. His expression was open with awe.

"That's how everyone should see it."

He turned to look at me, and I was suddenly aware of how close we were standing.

"You made it beautiful," he said.

"It already was." The words slipped out before I could filter them. "I just framed it differently."

August's gaze dropped to my mouth, then back to my eyes. This wasn't in the script. But the pull between us was undeniable.

"Sometimes the best shots are the ones you don't plan for." I couldn't believe I'd said such a clichéd line.

He leaned in slightly, and I moved toward him, drawn by something I couldn't—or refused to—name.

"Landon?" Felix's voice shattered the moment. "You should get lunch and then head to the next location. They'll be ready on time."

I stepped back. August cleared his throat.

"I'll be right there." I didn't take my eyes off August.

The interruption should have been a relief. This attraction was a complication I couldn't afford. Yet all I felt was frustration at having to leave.

"Felix is right. You should eat." He sounded disappointed.

I nodded. "Augie, I..." Shit. I'd just called him by the name only a few people used. "Will you be coming to set later?" That wasn't what I wanted to ask, but... Shit.

"Yeah." He didn't acknowledge the nickname. "Once Paige is back from her class."

I nodded and took another step back, trying to regain my professional composure. "Thank you. For today. For letting us use your store."

A small smile curved his lips. "Thanks for making it look like it belongs in a Christmas movie."

As I walked out into the bright July sunshine, I realized I was in dangerous territory. The almost-kiss would be something hanging between us until... when?

I was supposed to be directing a romance, not living one. And yet, for the first time since Thomas left, I found myself wanting to go off-script.

NINE

August

THE SATISFYING SCRAPE of my skate blades against freshly resurfaced ice echoed through the arena as I picked up speed. This was home—not just Pine Ridge, but the ice itself. It had always been my sanctuary when life got complicated, and right now, that word didn't begin to cover it.

Nick and I had the rink to ourselves for another half hour before the next reservation. We'd been going one-on-one for twenty minutes, pushing each other, trading goals, defensive moves, and trash talk in equal measure.

"Getting slow in your old age, Reeve," Nick taunted as he recovered and deked around my check, firing a wrist shot. It plinked off the right post, signaling a goal for him. With no goalie, we decided that you only scored if you were precise enough to hit one of the posts.

I retrieved the puck and skated behind the goal line. "That's big talk from someone who's six months older than me," I shot back.

Nick grinned, tapping his stick against the ice in that impatient rhythm that drove opposing defensemen crazy during games. "Age is a state of mind. And right now, your mind is somewhere else entirely."

He wasn't wrong.

Even as I settled the puck and prepared for another run, my thoughts drifted toward the shoot this morning. Landon standing close, showing me the playback of Declan and Brandon. The moment before Felix interrupted us.

I shook the memory away and focused, passing the puck to Nick as he skated backwards. He sent it right back as I charged forward. Crossing the blue line on the opposite side of the rink, I made my move, cutting sharply left. My backhand was strong, but my aim was off. The puck landed in the net instead of connecting with a post.

"Nice try." Nick's expression told me he was impressed by the attempt.

"If only there'd been a goalie there."

We laughed as Nick set up for another run at my goal. We played for ten more minutes until we were both breathing hard, shirts sticking to our backs. By unspoken agreement, we skated over to the bench for a break.

We stood side by side at the boards, squirting water into our mouths. "So, the developer situation. How bad is it? Shawn told me about the argument that happened while I was in Seattle."

I took another drink before answering. "Bad." I wiped sweat from my forehead with the back of my glove as I filled him in. "And yeah, I totally lost my temper in public yesterday. It's on social media. I'm surprised you didn't see it."

"I haven't watched. Sounds like you were justified, though."

"Still. Not my finest moment."

"You're fighting for your home. There's nothing to be ashamed of."

I stared out at the ice, at the place that had given me the launchpad for the career I had. "I don't even know where to start. There's no team here. It's just me and Paige and a few other business owners against a corporate machine."

Nick's shoulder bumped mine supportively. "I bet you've got more allies than you think, and that you could pull them together."

Mrs. Thompson's voice drifted through my mind, echoing her comments from the other day. "I appreciate that. It's so overwhelming, though. I wish I knew what would actually make a difference."

Nick took another long drink of water before shifting the topic. "So what's going on between you and the director?"

"Nothing." That came out too quick, but I wasn't ready to talk about what almost happened a few hours ago. Nick's cocked eyebrow made me sigh. I gave in because I could trust Nick not to judge. "Fine, okay. Maybe there's something." I shrugged.

"Shawn says the tension between you two could power the entire film set."

I laughed despite myself. "Your boyfriend has an active imagination."

"He also knows what he's talking about." Nick studied me. "Come on. We've been friends for years. I know when something's on your mind, and I think it's more than Donovan."

I took a deep breath. There was no real reason not to talk to Nick about this. "We almost kissed today. In the store, after filming. It was..."

Nick nodded, not looking surprised. "Why was it almost?"

"Felix interrupted us."

"So you do like him."

It wasn't a question. I dragged a hand through my sweaty hair.

"He's... complicated. Driven. Infuriating. But also... thoughtful." I paused, seeking the right words. "Yeah, there's something there. It makes no sense. And I can't stop thinking about him."

"Because it's inconvenient?"

"Because it's impossible." I rocked on my skates, fidgeting. "He lives in LA. I'm in Denver or here. He's in town for what? Two weeks total? Less now? How does that even work?"

Nick's expression softened. "Most of our friends who are coupled had the same concerns. Hell, Shawn and I certainly did."

"It's different." I tried to argue in my defense.

"Is it? Shawn travels for book tours and research. Then there's when he's in the zone or on deadline. Plus, I'm on the road half the year. On paper, we shouldn't work at all."

"But you do."

Nick smiled. "Because we decided that what we have is worth the effort. You've been fine with casual dating all these years because you haven't met someone who made you want to try for more." Nick put his hand on my shoulder and lowered his voice. "Question is, could Landon be worth it?"

The question hit harder than I expected. My

past relationships had always been uncomplicated by mutual agreement with whoever I was seeing. I'd wanted to keep the distractions minimal during the season. I also hadn't wanted to bring anyone home to Pine Ridge over the summer. So far, that had worked well and kept things easy.

But nothing about Landon Winslow was easy.

Before I could respond, the double doors to the rink opened, and a group of teenagers spilled in, geared up, carrying equipment bags and talking excitedly. They stopped in their tracks when they saw us.

"Oh wow. You two are here," Tia said as she skated over. "It's good to see you, Augie. Mr. Lawson, very cool to meet you. I'm Tia." We all traded fist bumps.

"Tia! I heard you had an outstanding season." I was happy to move to a different and much simpler topic.

Just a hint of blush crossed her cheeks. "Led the division in goals."

"Congrats," Nick said.

"I couldn't have done it without Augie and Coach Jacoby's guidance over the past couple of years."

I smiled, glad to know that I was able to help. "So you all are the seven o'clock?"

"Yeah," said a lanky boy whose name I couldn't remember. "They let us play when there are empty nights on the schedule."

"We'll get out of your way and let you get to it."

"Or, you could play with us," Tia said hopefully.

I looked at Nick, and he gave a nod. "Alright. Let's do it. You all warm up and I'll get me and Nick helmets."

"Is it cool if I stream this to show that we're getting to play with August Reeve and Nick Lawson?" Otto Thompson, whose dad owned the hardware store, asked as he held up his phone.

"Sure," I said, surprised by the request. "But it is just a pickup game."

"Yeah, but it's a pickup game with two NHL players," Otto said. "Jake's post with that Declan guy got, like, five hundred views. But this? Way cooler."

Within minutes, twelve teenagers had split themselves into teams and decided which of them would play with me and which with Nick. We deliberately played support roles in the 4-on-4 game, letting the kids take the lead and setting them up for plays.

We also coached in real time.

"Wider stance, Jake," I called as he kept losing his edge on turns. "Feel the inside of your blade."

"Katie, use your body to shield the puck," Nick

demonstrated during a stop in play, showing her how to position herself between the defender and the puck.

The kids soaked it up, their excitement palpable. A small crowd gathered in the stands. Word had spread about the game. Not only was there Otto's live stream, but a couple of the kids had friends in the stands with phones out.

"Man, I wish my dad's store was in the movie," Otto said, gulping water during a break. "He says the bakery's been packed since they filmed there."

"The film's good for the town," I agreed, my mind going back to Donovan and the council vote.

"I saw the pics you posted this morning when they were at your store," he said. "You had tons of comments. Did you really get to be in the movie?"

"Yeah. Paige and I got to be in the background." I'd taken a couple of behind-the-scenes shots while they were blocking, but hadn't looked at them since posting.

"I wish they had done the skating stuff with more people than just the kids. Was it cool getting to work on the hockey scenes?"

Before I could answer, Tia said the break was over, and we got back to the game.

In my first shift back on the ice, I was playing defense at the point, trying to get a puck from one of the teens. Movement in the stands caught my eye, and I saw Landon going up to take a seat alongside Shawn.

My breath caught as he sat down. He wore his customary black, and his gaze locked onto the ice. On me. Even from this distance, his intensity was unmistakable.

"Eyes on the puck, Reeve," Nick called as the teen took the puck from me. He made a quick pass to Nick to get it out of my reach and out of the zone.

I recovered quickly, skating hard to catch Nick. Knowing Landon was watching added extra urgency to my movements. I reached Nick just as he was about to pass, executing a perfect poke check that sent the puck sliding back toward center ice. Someone from my team got the puck and headed off on a breakaway that turned into a goal.

For the next fifteen minutes, I was hyperaware of Landon's presence as he and Shawn sat at the top of the bleachers. I played harder, sharper, showing my best while still letting the game stay about the teens. A part of me wanted to impress him. I wanted him to see this version of me.

When the game wound down, the teens clustered around us for final fist bumps and thank-yous. More phones were out, pictures taken, and promises made to do this again while Nick was still in town.

"That was awesome!" Otto said, beaming. "My friends are blowing up my phone. The stream's got tons of views already."

I smiled, clapping him on the shoulder. "You've got good instincts. Work on that slap shot and you'll be dangerous."

As the kids began dispersing, I allowed myself to look at Landon. He and Shawn were making their way down from the stands. I skated toward the exit, reaching it just as they approached.

"Hey." I was sweaty, my hair plastered to my forehead, and I knew how hockey players smelled after a game. None of this would add up to a good impression.

"That was outstanding to watch," Landon said, his voice more relaxed than usual.

"Thanks." I tried to find something else to say, but nothing came out.

"Nice to see you in your element."

"Yeah, well," I shrugged, unsure what to do with the admiration in his tone. "It was just a fun pickup game."

"It's not *just* anything," he countered. "I thought it was compelling to watch."

The compliment warmed me more than it should have. Nick joined us, giving a quick kiss to Shawn.

"How'd you know we were here?" Nick asked.

"Social media." Shawn grinned. "The impromptu game has gone mini-viral, at least locally. Someone tagged me in a comment."

"Seriously?" I glanced at the thinning crowd, noticing more phones than I'd realized, some still pointed in our direction.

Landon nodded. "Felix showed it to me when we'd wrapped shooting on Main Street."

An awkward silence fell between us. We hadn't talked much when I was on set during the afternoon shoot. Since I'd been an observer, I stayed quiet. But now, it was like I didn't know how to act around him at all.

"We were thinking about grabbing dinner at The Keg." Nick broke the moment. "You two want to join?"

"I can't," Landon said almost before Nick had finished asking. "I need to prep for tomorrow's scenes." His eyes met mine. "We're shooting the tree-trimming scene at the Nash cabin."

"I know," I said. "I'm planning to come by."

Another loaded silence, charged with possibility. It made me second-guess my decision to go tomorrow. It'd be a very romantic scene.

"Good," he finally said. "Your input has been...

valuable." He stepped back, nodding to Shawn and Nick. "I should go."

With a final glance at me, he turned and walked away.

I watched him go, oddly deflated. But it seemed that he wanted me to be there tomorrow.

"Wow," Shawn said as soon as Landon was out of earshot. "That was something."

"What was?" I asked.

"That." Shawn pointed between me and the retreating figure of Landon. "Trust me. The way he was watching you? That wasn't just professional curiosity."

Nick squeezed Shawn's shoulder. "Leave him alone. He'll figure it out."

But I was only half-listening. My gaze followed Landon as he walked out of the rink and into the parking lot. The pull between us was getting stronger, more impossible to ignore.

Maybe I should ask Shawn if he could script the next scene for me and Landon.

TEN

Landon

INSIDE THE LOG cabin we'd rented for the shoot, everything was a sensory lie, just like everything else in the room. The fire in the hearth was a flicker of gas-fed flames behind fake logs. The snow drifting past the window was a slow cascade of biodegradable material. Worst of all, the intimacy between my two lead actors wasn't working.

We were on hour three of shooting Scene 45: "The Tree-Trimming Confession." It was the emotional turning point of the movie. Logistically simple, emotionally Herculean.

Callum and Julian, stranded by the convenient snowstorm, decorate a sparse Christmas tree with makeshift ornaments. The playful activity is supposed to dissolve into a moment of profound vulnerability, where Callum confesses the real, painful reason he fled New York. It required a delicate, simmering chemistry. What I was getting was as warm and spontaneous as a tax audit.

"Brandon, you're not listening to him." I kept my voice as calm as possible. I was watching on a monitor, my hands clenched tight. "He's telling you he's afraid his career might force him away from the only home he's ever known. Your character should be connecting that to his own sense of displacement. I need to see that empathy. Right now, you look like you're trying to remember your next line."

Brandon Atkins, a man who'd built his television fame on charming smirks, ran a hand through his perfectly coiffed hair. "I'm feeling it, Lan. I really am."

"Then show me." I struggled to keep frustration out of my voice. "Action is behavior. If you're feeling it, your body will show it. You're holding that string of popcorn like it's a dead snake. It's an olive branch. An excuse to be close to him. Use it."

Declan Thorne, despite this being his first romantic role, was doing a good job. He'd improved light years since the skating scenes. He was delivering his lines about being traded with a sort of earnest, puppy-dog sadness that was playing well on camera. But he was acting in a vacuum. Brandon was sucking all the energy out of the moment.

I stood up from my chair and joined the actors at the tree. "Remember the scene on the ice? Remember how it felt for Julian when he stumbled into Callum's arms? That physical connection created emotional truth." I positioned myself in front of Declan, mimicking his blocking. "When Callum shares his fear, you connect that to losing your fiancé, about how you designed buildings meant to last centuries but couldn't build a relationship that would last a year. You don't just hear Callum's words —you feel them."

I demonstrated, letting my face register a flicker of recognition, of shared pain. It was easy enough to bring up memories of what went wrong with Thomas. "The popcorn string is just a prop, but it represents this fragile, temporary connection you're building together. That's your character's reality."

From the edge of the set, beyond the lights, August watched. He'd been there since we started, leaning against the cottage's back wall, a silent, solid presence. After the past day, his quiet observation seemed far more personal, like he was trying to figure me out. The thought, like the memories of my rela-tionship failure, was a distraction I was failing to tune out.

"Let's go again." I rubbed my temples as I returned to the monitor. "From the top of the scene."

The crew shifted as the tension on set ratcheted up. They could sense my patience was running out despite my best efforts. Felix was giving me his patented "let's just breathe" look. I didn't know why, but this scene was falling flat even though the two were perfect in the meet-cute and the other scenes we'd shot yesterday.

Maybe it was me. The scene was a testament to everything I secretly believed about romance. It was a performance. A series of gestures and lines designed to create an illusion. And when the actors weren't good enough, you saw through the artifice. Was I seeing flaws that didn't actually exist?

The pressure of *Silo* was on my mind too. If I couldn't even make two handsome actors look like they were falling in love, how could I deliver with the stark, brutal honesty of my own film?

Before I called for action, out of the corner of my eye, I saw August push off the wall and slip out a side door. I missed his presence already even though he hadn't given any opinions today. Although, I didn't ask for any either. I guessed that he didn't believe in this attempt at Christmas magic either.

We ran the scene again... and again... and again.

"No, cut, cut!" I threw my hands up in defeat.

"It's not working. Brandon, you're anticipating the kiss. Declan, you're telegraphing the comfort. We're not earning the moment."

Frustration crept into my voice. "The whole point of this scene is the subtext. You're talking about hockey and architecture, but you're really talking about being lost. You're two lonely people finding connection in a world that doesn't make sense."

"I'm just not..." Brandon looked helpless.

I turned away, running a hand over my face. "Let's call it a wrap on this scene for today. We'll pick it up in the morning."

It wouldn't throw the schedule off too much if we could come back and get it right first thing. We were still shooting in the cabin tomorrow, so I'd make it work.

A collective sigh of relief passed through the crew. I walked past Felix, who knew me well enough not to say a word.

Outside, the sun was nearly down, and the sky was a deep purple. As I headed toward Main Street, the decorations we'd strung up came into view. They were lit up and sparkling—a cheerful mockery of the mess I'd left behind.

All I wanted was to go back to my B&B, open my laptop, and lose myself in *Silo* and its world of lonely landscapes and unspoken truths. A world I understood, without forced yuletide cheer and counterfeit emotions.

As I walked, each storefront I passed reminded me how this town had transformed into a film set. Mrs. Miller's bakery window, now framed with plastic holly. The hardware store's door, adorned with a wreath.

In the quiet of the evening, Pine Ridge seemed suspended between its authentic self and the fantasy version we'd imposed on it. I understood that feeling all too well. The constant tension between who you are and who you present yourself to be.

My mind churned with the day's failure as people passed me by. Some of them I recognized, but others I didn't. No one spoke to me, and I avoided making direct eye contact. I didn't want to project my bad mood any more than I already had.

The issue wasn't the actors or the script. The problem was that I was asking them to fake something I'd forgotten how to feel myself. After Thomas left, I'd built a lot of walls. I directed my own life like a scene. And now I pushed Brandon and Declan to show me feelings that I'd wanted nothing to do with.

And there he was.

August.

Augie. Had I really called him that?

He was standing in front of Reeve's Textiles, a

ring of old-fashioned keys in his hand, locking up for the night. The store was dark behind him, but the colored lights strung across the awning bathed him in a soft, nostalgic glow. He looked like a figure from a different era.

I should have gone the other way. But I wanted to talk to him. It was an illogical impulse. One I couldn't resist.

He turned, and our eyes locked. His expression was neutral in the dim light, but I caught the shift in his posture that reminded me of the moment we had stepped back from each other. The moment of the almost-kiss had burned itself into my brain.

"Did you get the scene?"

"No." I sighed and leaned against the wood planks of the storefront. "You were smart to get out when you did. I spent the last two hours pushing two actors to show me they were feeling something."

I hadn't meant to vent, but the words came tumbling out.

"It's a fool's errand trying to manufacture a connection." I looked past him to the decorations down the street. "You can't script chemistry. You can't light it or block it. It's either there, or it's not. My job is to fake it when it's not. And today, I just... couldn't."

August was quiet for a long moment. He finished

locking the door, turned, and leaned against the door, mirroring my posture. Under the Christmas lights, the usual wariness in his eyes now looked like concern.

"Maybe you're trying too hard."

"It's my job to try *too hard*."

"Is it? The stuff at the rink. What you shot here. It worked because it was real. You can't fake how a skate catches an edge. You can't fake gravity. Same thing with that first moment of connection." He paused, and the pull I felt when I was near him kicked into overdrive. "Maybe this isn't something you can fake, either. Maybe you just have to create a space where something real has a chance to happen."

I let out a short, harsh laugh. "This is Hollywood. We don't leave things to chance. We build the house, we furnish it, and we tell the actors where to stand when they declare their undying love."

"Sounds exhausting."

"It is." The admission surprised me as I said it.

We stood in comfortable silence, the only sounds being the faint chirp of crickets and the low buzz of music from the band playing at The Keg.

"The story is simple enough," I finally said. "Architect with a broken heart meets a hometown hero who is also lost. They get snowed in, they connect, fall in love, the end. You've probably seen that movie dozens of times."

"I have. And I love it every single time." The smile that formed on his face made my heart leap. "It's easier in the movies, though. The solutions are cleaner. You make a grand gesture at a gazebo and everything's fixed." He shook his head, and his expression sobered. "Real life is messier. You've got developers and town councils and a century of history you're trying not to let turn into a parking lot."

I grunted out an agreement. "Or you're struggling to direct a romance when you can't even successfully be in one yourself. Not to mention that the movie is the ticket to the one you really want to make. I'm not sure there's a grand gesture that can solve either of our problems."

The lines between the fake movie plot and real life, between my professional frustrations and his personal struggles, were disappearing fast.

I took him in. The faint scar on his jaw, the worn-in softness of his t-shirt, the lights reflecting in his eyes. He wasn't a character to be directed.

He shifted, turning to face me more directly. "Yeah. We're left without the holiday movie guarantee. We have to risk everything without knowing how it'll turn out."

He looked at me with such intensity that my pulse sped up.

In that moment, standing under the glow of the Christmas lights, everything else fell away. I was just a man standing next to another man who made me feel seen for the first time in a very long time.

I pushed off the wall. "Augie." My voice was just above a whisper.

He looked at me with a questioning expression as I took a step to close the space between us.

Before he could speak, before I could think, I put my hand on his chest. I felt the steady beat of his heart. Cupping his jaw, my thumb brushed over the line of the scar. His eyes widened in surprise as his lips parted slightly.

Anticipation hung in the air—like the moment before calling "action."

I leaned in and kissed him.

It wasn't a soft, movie-style kiss. It was desperate and hungry. All of the tension and frustration and longing that had been building since I first saw him and we argued about a quilt rack poured into that kiss. His lips were firm and warm, and for a split second, he was still.

Then, a low moan rumbled in his chest, and he kissed me back.

His hand came up to the back of my head, and

he pulled me closer. His other arm wrapped around my waist, pulling me in. He was stronger than I expected. I gave myself over to him, letting go of the control I clung to so desperately.

For the first time in a long while, I wasn't thinking. It was all feeling. The taste of him, the rough scrape of his evening stubble, the solid wall of his body, the way he seemed to pour all of himself into the kiss.

It was messy and reckless... and everything I wanted.

We broke apart, breathless. My hand was still on his chest. His eyes were dark, searching my face as if trying to find an explanation for what had just happened. I had none to give.

"Landon."

I didn't know what to say. I had no idea where we might go from here. All I knew was that this connection was the most unplanned and terrifyingly perfect moment I'd ever had.

ELEVEN

August

My mind had been a relentless replay reel all night, a chaotic loop of Christmas lights and the shocking, undeniable rightness of Landon's mouth on mine. It wasn't a gentle, exploratory kiss. It had been a collision, a frantic, desperate act that had left me feeling like I'd just played a triple-overtime game. My whole body vibrated with the aftershocks.

Who was this man who could kiss me with such raw hunger? The director in him was a controlling perfectionist. The man I'd sat with in the park was quiet and empathetic. And the man who'd kissed me... he was a complete unknown.

I drove to the cabin with the windows down. The cool morning air did nothing to clear my head. I didn't know what to expect. Would he pretend it never happened? Would he be the cold, dismissive director again? Would we talk about it?

I spotted him the instant I walked into the cabin. He was in his usual black, standing beside the camera, talking in low, intense tones to the DP. He gave off tense vibes, a stark contrast to the man who I'd held in my arms for that one breathless moment.

He glanced up, his eyes sweeping the set. For a fraction of a second, his gaze landed on me. I couldn't read the emotions that crossed his face before he shifted to a blank expression. He turned back to his conversation without a word of acknowledgment.

Okay. So that was how it was going to be. Avoidance.

The crew, accustomed to Landon's moods, tiptoed around him, but I caught Felix watching, his features tightened in concern and exasperation.

I fell into a chat with Brandon and Declan. They seemed at ease, which was a contrast to how everyone else was. Given how much trouble this scene caused them yesterday, it was refreshing to find them calm. As we talked about what Pine Ridge actually looks like at Christmas versus the movie's decorations, Landon snapped, halting everything.

"Reeve! My trailer. Now."

The entire set fell silent. Declan and Brandon winced. Crew members became very interested in whatever piece of equipment was closest to them.

I felt a dozen pairs of eyes on me as I followed him. We exited through the cabin's front door and walked the twenty yards to his trailer. He moved quickly and put distance between us. He opened the door with such force that I thought it might fly off the hinges.

I managed to keep my calm, and when I stepped in, I gently pulled it shut. I tried to prepare myself for whatever he had to say.

He was pacing. Four steps one way, four steps back.

"Last night was a mistake," he said without preamble. He studied his wall of scheduling cards.

I stayed by the door, crossing my arms over my chest. I wasn't surprised. It was the predictable move. "Was it?"

"Of course it was." He spun around to face me. His blue eyes blazed with a defensive energy. "It was unprofessional, and it complicates everything. One, I am the director of this film." He held up a finger for each point as he made it. "Two, you are a consultant on my project. Three, this film will wrap in six days, after which I will return to Los Angeles, and you will, I assume, return to your life in Pine

Ridge and then Denver. Ergo, any… extracurricular activity is a pointless complication with no viable future."

He finished his speech looking at me as if he expected a round of applause for his unassailable logic.

I watched him for a beat, letting the silence hang in the air. "You left out number four," I said quietly.

He frowned. "Number four?"

"It was the best I've been kissed in a very long time."

The color drained from his face, clearly not expecting a counterargument. He opened his mouth, then closed it again. He was a man who'd built his life on having the right words, and I had rendered him speechless with a single sentence.

"But you're right about those first three." I moved toward him, and he shifted back. "I know you're leaving, and there's a thousand or so miles between us. And, believe me, I've got my own list of reasons why kissing you was a terrible idea."

I closed the remaining gap between us, trapping him between me and the corkboard. "But it happened. Walking around pretending it didn't is a hell of a lot more exhausting than just admitting it." I lowered my voice. "So the question isn't whether it was a mistake. The real thing we have to figure out is what are we going to do about it while we've still got time?"

He stared at me, his eyes wide, his defenses stripped away. I saw the battle within him.

"We stop." His tone was uncertain. "We maintain a professional relationship until the film wraps. And then we go our separate ways."

It was the sensible choice. The smart one. It would save us both from any hurt down the line.

"Is that what you want?" I held his gaze, refusing to let him look away. I saw the answer in the slight tremor of his lips, in the way his Adam's apple bobbed as he swallowed.

He couldn't say it. He couldn't lie. Not to me. Not now.

I exhaled slowly. "So here's another option. We both know this comes with an expiration date. There are no illusions here, no gazebos, no happily ever afters." He flinched at my use of words from last night. "So what if we don't fight it? What if, for the next six days, we stop pretending there's nothing between us?"

It was a reckless proposal. A pact to indulge in something we know from the start won't last. Even for me, someone who had years of satisfying casual relationships, it wasn't the ideal outcome. Still, I wanted all the time I could get with Landon.

He stared at me, his face full of conflict. I could almost hear the gears of his brain grinding, weighing the pros and cons. He was a man who storyboarded his life into neat little squares. I was asking him to improvise.

"No promises. Just this." I pointed between him and me. "Until the last scene is shot."

He closed his eyes for a long moment. When he opened them again, the frantic energy was gone, replaced by a kind of calm resignation. He knew the risks but was going to take the leap anyway.

"Okay." He sighed and ran a hand over the stubble on his cheek. "Okay."

The tension in the trailer didn't disappear, but it transformed from awkward to anticipation. We'd made a deal.

I reached out and tucked a stray strand of dark hair behind his ear, my fingers brushing against his skin. He shivered at the slight contact. "Good," I said. "Now that we've settled that..." I let my hand drop. "My place. Tonight. After you wrap. It's more private than your B&B."

He understood what the offer meant immediately. His gaze flickered with a fresh wave of uncertainty, but he held my eye and gave a single, sharp nod. "I'd like that."

My house was a simple three-bedroom craftsman I bought a few years back and furnished to make it comfortable. But with Landon on the way, the worn leather couch, the bookshelf stuffed with everything from hockey biographies to spy novels, even the framed picture of my family at Paige's graduation—all of it seemed like it was on display.

Tonight, my home felt like a set.

I'd showered and changed into clean jeans and a t-shirt, and now I was pacing my living room just like Landon had paced in his trailer. My heart thudded with a nervous energy I hadn't felt before a hookup in years. But this wasn't just a hookup. This was Landon. And that made it more.

Just after nine, headlights swept across the front window. I watched as Landon's rental car pulled into the driveway. He got out and stood there for a moment, looking at my house as if it were a new location to scout.

He walked up the short sidewalk, his steps hesitant. I opened the door before he could knock.

"Hey," I said, trying to keep my voice casual.

"Hey." He had a bottle of wine in his hand, a ridiculously expensive-looking red. It was such a formal gesture that it made me smile.

"Come in." I stepped back.

His eyes took everything in with that familiar, critical sweep. But this time it wasn't about aesthetics or shot composition. He was taking me in. He scanned the bookshelf, the framed photos of my family, the embroidery on the walls, the stack of dog-eared paperbacks on the coffee table, the small Christmas tree I'd taken out of the attic a couple days ago and placed on top.

"This is nice," he said, his voice quiet.

"It's home." I took the wine from him. "Thanks for this, but I was thinking something a little stronger." I led him to the kitchen and pulled two glasses and a bottle of whiskey from the cupboard. I poured two fingers into each and handed one to him.

He took it, his fingers brushing mine. The same jolt as last night shot through me. We stood in the quiet of my kitchen, the silence stretching, charged with everything our pact implied.

He took a small sip of his whiskey. "So, this is the part where we...?" He trailed off, looking at me with uncertainty in his eyes.

It was time to take action. "This is the part where we stop talking."

I took the glass from his hand and set it on the counter next to mine. I put my hands on his hips, drawing him in slowly, giving him every opportunity to back away.

He didn't.

He let me pull him against me. He rested his hands on my chest.

"Augie." The roughness of his voice sent shivers down my spine.

I didn't answer with words but by claiming his mouth. This kiss was nothing like the frantic collision of last night. It was slow and deliberate. I took my time, learning the shape of his lips, the taste of him mixed with whiskey.

He groaned, a soft, yielding sound, and melted against me. For a man who lived his life in a state of absolute control, it was the ultimate act of surrender.

I broke the kiss and trailed my lips along his jaw, to a sensitive spot just below his ear. He shuddered, clutching at my shirt.

"My whole life is about telling people what to do." His voice was thick with need. "Where to stand. What to feel." He tilted his head, giving me better access. "I don't... I don't want to be in charge right now."

That admission hit me harder than any physical touch. It was an act of trust and vulnerability. He was offering me his most prized possession: his control.

I didn't take that lightly.

"Okay," I whispered against his skin. "I've got you."

I scooped him up. He let out a startled gasp as he wrapped his arms around my neck. He was lighter than I expected, lean but solid. I carried him out of the kitchen and down the short hallway to my bedroom, which was lit only by the white Christmas lights I'd strung along the window.

I laid him gently on my bed, and I joined him, bracing my weight on my forearms, caging him in. His eyes were huge in the dim light, watching me with a mix of desire and uncertainty that sent flutters through my chest.

Piece by piece, I undressed him. With every layer of his black clothes that I stripped away, it felt like I was peeling back a layer of his defenses. The designer t-shirt revealed lean shoulders and sharp collarbones that I traced with my mouth. Working my way down his chest, lightly dusted with fine dark hairs, I spread light kisses as my hands wandered over him.

The fitted jeans along with his briefs slid down his hips, letting me follow the trail of dark hair that went down from his navel. He was hard, waiting for my touch. It wasn't time for that just yet, though.

Once I had him stripped, I took my time memorizing his body with my hands and mouth, learning the places that made him gasp, the spots that made him arch into my touch. I focused only on his pleasure and making him let go.

He trembled when I flicked my tongue over his left nipple. "Jesus, Augie..."

"Oh yeah," I murmured against his skin. My hands drifted lower, fingers tangling in the dark curls at the base of his shaft.

Landon lived in his head, but I was determined to overwhelm his brain with pure sensation.

I moved down to his cock, which I could no longer resist. It stood proudly, waiting for its turn. I wrapped my lips around him, taking him deep, my tongue tracing the thick vein underneath.

His hips came off the bed, a shocked groan sounding from his throat. I kept him there, sucking hard, hollowing my cheeks until he was panting, fingers clawing at the sheets.

"God, yes, like that, just like—"

His voice broke when I pressed lightly behind his balls. His whole body went rigid, breathing ragged.

"Augie...Yes... More."

I eased a finger inside him, slicked with his own precum. His eyes flew wide, brilliant blue and shockingly vulnerable. It was intimate as his body yielded reluctantly, then hungrily to my advances. A second joined the first, curling deep. He cried out, arching, sending his dick down my throat.

"You taste so good," I said when I pulled off. "And you're so fucking hot like this."

He gasped my name, writhing. The desperate hunger on his face and the way his hands fisted the comforter were all the encouragement I needed to keep going. I took him deep, and when I curled my fingers just right, my reward was precum flowing onto my tongue.

He was close, trembling on the edge, his thighs shaking against me.

"No," he choked out, pushing my head back from his hardness. His eyes went wild. "Not like this." He swallowed hard, his chest heaving. "I want you. All of you. Inside me." His gaze locked with mine, intense and demanding. "Fuck me, Augie. Now."

It was the most beautiful request I'd ever heard.

I freed my fingers slowly. His cock was flushed and dripping. I kissed him hard.

"Need lube," I said as I moved to find the bottle in my nightstand. I slicked myself with a thick dollop that made him groan as he watched. He took it from me, squirting some onto his own fingers, reaching to prep himself.

I grabbed a condom from the drawer and rolled it

down my length, the latex cool and snug. Landon's gaze was hot and focused. I settled between his legs, and he shifted to give me a better position.

Pushing in slowly, I allowed his body to stretch while I adjusted to his incredible heat and tight resistance. He let out a sharp, ragged breath, his eyes fluttering shut. His face tightened, jaw clenching. I paused, letting him breathe as sweat beaded on his forehead.

"Okay?" I asked, my voice rough.

He nodded. "Just... give me a second. Damn, you're big." A faint smile touched his lips. "So good."

I ran my hands over his chest, caressing him. "It's all yours. When you're ready."

He moaned long and opened his eyes. The look he gave me was one of raw, unguarded need. "Move. Please. Now."

Our rhythm was slow at first, deep rolls of my hips. With every stroke, I watched the tension melt further from his body, replaced by a dazed pleasure. His hands rested on my shoulders as he used his legs to pull me deeper.

"Faster," he gasped. "Harder. Want all of you."

I obliged, driving into him with increasing force, the sound of skin against skin loud in the quiet room. He met me thrust for thrust, his body arching, his cock leaking onto his belly. His breath came in sharp, rhythmic gasps that matched my thrusts.

His groans were low and guttural. "Yes... oh god, Augie... right there!"

"I love hearing you say my name," I grunted out between thrusts.

The bed creaked beneath us. Sweat slicked our bodies together. He felt incredible—tight and hot, clenching around me. I lost myself in the sounds he made, and the way his body moved with mine.

His hands fisted in the sheets again, knuckles white. "Close... so close..." His voice was tight. He wrapped his hand around his hardness and jerked it fiercely a couple of times before he came across his stomach and onto his chest. "Fuck yes!"

Watching him come apart shattered the last of my control. His hole spasmed around my shaft, and the hot, rhythmic clench was too much. My climax ripped through me a moment later, leaving me shaking as I shot a huge load.

I collapsed onto him, my head buried in the curve of his neck. We stayed like that for a long time, tangled together, breathing hard. His fingers traced lazy patterns on my back.

"What are you thinking about?" I rolled off of him, took care of the condom, and then snuggled up against his side.

He was silent for a moment. "This isn't how I thought this day would go when I woke up this morning. It wasn't in the script."

I chuckled. "No?"

"No." He turned under my arm to face me, his expression serious in the dim light. "I was planning to avoid you. To pretend last night didn't happen. To bury myself in work."

"But I didn't let you do that."

He studied my face. "No. You didn't. Now I'm here. In your bed." His honesty was disarming. "I'm thinking about how we have less than six days, and how that's both not enough time and probably more than we should risk."

I pushed the date aside, focusing on him next to me. "Let's not waste it, then."

He nodded, his eyes holding mine.

"I'm glad you're here," I said simply.

Landon gave me a tender smile. "Me too. Let's make the most of this."

TWELVE

Landon

For a disorienting moment, I didn't know where I was. The bed didn't feel familiar, yet it was possibly the most comfortable I'd ever been in.

I opened my eyes.

I was in Augie's room. Beside me, he slept on his stomach, one arm draped over my waist in a gesture of casual possession. His brown hair was a mess, and stubble ran along his jaw and cheeks. I'd never seen him look more relaxed.

A cold spike of anxiety, sharp and familiar, pierced the warm, hazy comfort. Waking up in someone else's bed, in someone else's life, was a breach of protocol. My first impulse was to slide out from under his arm, gather my clothes, and retreat.

But I didn't move. The weight of his arm held me there. And, if I was being honest, so did a profound reluctance to break the spell. Last night had been a surrender. Running now would be a betrayal of what we'd agreed to.

My eyes scanned his room, a space that radiated comfort and personal history. A well-crafted wooden dresser stood against one wall, its surface adorned with a hockey championship trophy. Several photographs of teammates surrounded it. It was a younger Augie—college, maybe. A worn quilt, clearly handmade, sat folded at the foot of the bed. The walls held a few framed photos and paintings with landscapes of the Cascades and from Pine Ridge. Across the big window, white Christmas lights glowed.

The room wasn't curated or designed. It wasn't a set. In fact, it reminded me of why the art department didn't want to use props in his store. Reality was better.

For all of Thomas's arguments that I directed our life, he had been methodical about our mornings in our old Silver Lake apartment. The blinds were calibrated to let in exactly the right amount of light. The espresso machine started precisely at 6:30. His running clothes were always laid out the night before.

Augie stirred, a low mumble escaping his lips, and tightened his arm around me, snuggling closer to me. He was a human furnace, radiating steady, comforting heat. I should have felt trapped. Thomas was never a cuddler. Truth was that I liked the feel of him against me.

I lay there for what felt like a long time, just breathing. This stillness was a foreign country. My mind was always moving. But in the quiet of Augie's bedroom, there was nothing to solve. It was a single, perfect, static shot, and I didn't want to call "cut."

His lips brushed against my shoulder, a sleepy, unconscious kiss. "Mmm, you're awake." His voice was a low, gravelly rumble.

"I am."

He nuzzled my neck, his stubble pleasantly rough against my skin. "Regrets?"

It was a test. I knew it. He was giving me an out. The logical part of my brain screamed at me to take it.

"None."

He was quiet for a moment. Then he pressed a more deliberate kiss to my shoulder. "Good." He unwrapped himself from me, and I missed his touch.

He sat up, stretching, his back a landscape of muscle in the morning light. "Coffee?"

The question was so normal, so domestic, it threw me off balance. "Yes, please."

We dressed in our boxers and t-shirts from the night before. In the kitchen, I leaned against the counter while he moved around, brewing coffee, getting mugs, offering sugar and milk.

The mug he handed me wished a "Happy Ho-ho-hockey Christmas." Augie had one with forest animals playing hockey next to a decorated tree.

"You're taking Christmas in July seriously, I see."

"I couldn't help it." The faintest hint of pink colored his cheeks. "I don't normally decorate this place because I'm only in town for a couple of days, and then I'm staying with Paige because she's living in the house we grew up in. But with all the Christmas in town, I pulled out a few things here. I like the bit of festiveness it adds to the place."

I found it delightful that he loved the movie magic so much that he wanted some of it here. "So do I. Cheers." I raised my mug. He did the same, and we clinked them together.

As we drank, we didn't talk about last night. We didn't talk about the deal we'd made. I told him about my attempts at trying to cook and failing. He told me a story about his grandmother's stew, the recipe for which he was still trying to perfect because it never tasted quite like he and Paige remembered it.

It was such a simple scene that if I had tried to write it, I would have dismissed it as too on-the-nose.

"How about I make us breakfast?" he said, opening his refrigerator. "Eggs, bacon, toast. Nothing fancy, but it'll be good."

I nodded, sipping my coffee. "I'd like that. Do you mind if I take a few minutes to freshen up?"

He flashed me a smile over his shoulder as he gathered ingredients. "Of course. Make yourself at home."

The phrase was casual, but I couldn't help but wonder what it might be like to make a home with him.

Before I made it to the bathroom, a half-open door caught my eye, one I hadn't noticed last night. Curiosity pulled me toward it.

I looked inside to a sunlit room that felt like it belonged to a different home. It was a workspace, but unlike any I'd ever seen. Wood cabinets lined the walls, their small drawers labeled in a neat script. A large table dominated the center, its surface clear except for a wooden hoop holding taut fabric. But what took my breath away were the colors.

Threads. Maybe hundreds of them. Organized in a massive color wheel on one wall, the gradients shifted with breathtaking precision from the deepest midnight blue through aquamarine to pale sky, then into greens, yellows, reds, purples. It was a textile rainbow, capturing the entire visible spectrum.

I moved closer to the table, drawn to the hoop. Inside it was an in-progress piece—an image emerging from countless tiny, precise stitches. I recognized it immediately. It was Pine Ridge's town square, but not as it normally looked. It was our set with the fake snow and holiday lights surrounded by the equipment. In thread form, it took on a strange, magical quality.

"AR," I murmured. There'd been several small, framed pieces at Reeve's Textiles, signed with those simple initials. Was it him?

"Found my secret." Augie's voice, coming from the doorway, startled me. When I turned, he was leaning against the frame, a dish towel thrown over his shoulder.

"I didn't mean to snoop." I suddenly felt like I'd intruded on something private.

He shook his head, a small smile playing on his lips. "It's fine. I'm not ashamed of it. Just not something that fits neatly into the hockey player image." He came into the room, moving to stand beside me. "My Aunt Rose taught me when I was a kid because I was fascinated watching her make intricate images out of thread. But then it became..." He trailed off, his fingers lightly touching the edge of the hoop.

"An escape." I finished for him.

He looked at me, surprise flickering in his eyes. "Yeah. When things get too much in my head, this helps. It's meditative. The repetition. The focus." He picked up a needle threaded with pale gold and went back to work. "One stitch at a time. Building something bigger."

I watched as he made a few stitches, adding a gleam to one of the strings of light on the gazebo. It was hypnotic, watching as he passed the thread through the fabric. His hands—which I'd seen holding hockey sticks, curled into fists, and claiming my body—were gentle and precise. The juxtapositions were startling.

"It's a different kind of creation," I said, thinking aloud. "Film is collaborative, chaotic. A thousand moving pieces all trying to align. This is solitary. Patient."

"Both tell stories." He looked up. "Just their own languages."

I looked at the piece again. The town square, transformed by our production, now being transformed again through his hands. "This is beautiful. I hope you'll show it to me when it's finished."

I was seeing Augie through fresh eyes. This artistic soul beneath the hockey player was like discovering a subplot I'd missed in my own film. I'd been so quick to categorize him, to frame him as the stubborn small-town hockey hero. But he was far more than that.

I wanted to know all of him. How was I going to say goodbye when the shoot was done?

"Breakfast is probably burning," he said suddenly, setting down the needle. "Come on. We can talk about my hobby later."

"I know you might not have wanted to share it, but I'm glad I know this part of you."

A faint blush colored his cheeks, and he ducked his head as we returned to the kitchen.

Luckily, breakfast was fine. Augie slid bacon and eggs onto plates while I poured more coffee. The domesticity should have felt stifling, but it was anything but.

"So, what's on the agenda for today?" He asked as he put a small plate of toast between us at the island. "I haven't looked at the call sheet yet."

"This evening and tonight we'll be shooting. Everyone is taking a few hours off this morning before setting up." I shrugged. "After the past couple of days, Felix decided we all needed to catch our breath."

Augie's eyebrows rose. "That rough, huh?"

"Yeah." I hated my role in making it as bad as it

was, which was why I let Felix make the call. I trust him to get us wrapped on time.

"Well, in that case," he said, with a glint in his eye, "I want to show you something. If you're up for it?"

"What is it?"

"A place. My place. Not this house—though this is mine too." His smile grew. "Somewhere that matters to me."

I wasn't about to turn down more time with Augie. "Yes. I'd like that."

Augie's "place" required a forty-minute drive into the mountains, then another fifteen hiking up a steep, wooded trail. He moved with easy familiarity through the terrain, while I picked my way cautiously over roots and rocks. My designer sneakers were inadequate for this, but I made do.

But when we emerged from the tree line, the journey was immediately worthwhile.

The view was staggering. We stood on a rocky promontory, the entire valley spread below us like a vast green quilt. Pine Ridge was a tiny cluster of buildings in the distance, a miniature model of itself. Beyond it, the landscape rolled away in endless waves of forest and mountain, a breathtaking scale that made human concerns seem trivial.

"Wow." The word didn't describe the scene, but it was all I had.

"Yeah," August said, his voice quiet beside me. "I've been coming here for years. Whenever things felt too big. This view puts everything back into perspective."

We sat on a large, flat rock, our shoulders nearly touching. Cool, sharp air carried the scent of pine. The silence was a comfortable shared space that didn't need to be filled. I was a man who lived by words, by scripts and dialogue, but with Augie, the quiet moments didn't compel me to speak.

I thought of the embroidery room. Of his hands making those tiny, perfect stitches. Of the town square he'd captured. He was an artist too. He saw the world as it was, but also how it could be. That's what had drawn me to directing—the power to reshape reality, to find the beauty in the ordinary.

"The scene in the cabin," Augie said, his voice thoughtful, "I haven't seen you push that hard with character work. The rink sequence worked because of all the physical action and needing that right. But in the cabin, what were you seeing that felt wrong?"

It was clear he wasn't just asking a filmmaking question. He was holding a door open for me. I could walk through it, or I could pretend I didn't see it and stick to the artistic point of view. After last night, I felt an unexpected compulsion to surrender something more. My story.

"You should know that I apologized to them both. I was putting too much of myself in that moment and the care I wish I'd taken with a relationship in the past."

Unable to meet his eyes, I looked toward the stars instead. "I've got this passion project called *Silo*. It's a stark, black-and-white drama about a farmer in the Dust Bowl. I've spent years writing it, obsessing over every detail. It was all I talked about. All I thought about."

I stole a look at him and found him watching.

"I was with someone at the time. His name was Thomas. A scenic designer making a reputation for himself. Kind. Supportive. Or, he tried to be." I let out a humorless laugh. "The more obsessed I got with the film, the more distant he became. He said I was treating our relationship like a subplot to be directed. Something to be handled when I had a spare moment, but not the A-story. The A-story was always the movie."

I paused, remembering the way Thomas had looked on that last day. Standing in our apartment, suitcase by the door, afternoon sunlight streaming through the windows. It would've made a beautiful shot—perfect lighting for romantic devastation. Even in that moment, I'd been framing it.

"My parents were like that too." The words flowed more freely now. "My father's law practice always came first. My mother's charity work always took precedence. They were successful, respected, and separate. I grew up thinking that was normal. That achievement required sacrifice. That you chose your passion, and everything else was secondary."

August listened without interruption, even when I took a pause. He sensed I wasn't done.

"The night I finally finished the draft of *Silo*, I was euphoric. I felt like I had created something special. I handed it to Thomas, expecting him to be as excited as I was. Instead, he packed a bag. He told me he couldn't compete with a screenplay. He said I wanted a producer, not a partner. Someone to fund my life, both emotionally and financially, while I focused on my art."

I ran my hand through my hair and stared out at the landscape.

"That's why I made a rule." My voice was flat. "Keep them separate. Career and relationships. They're two different projects that require their own skill sets. They can't coexist. One will always cannibalize the other. Between the romance in the movie and... whatever this is." I looked back at him and pointed between us. "It's brought all of that back, and I took that out on people who deserved better."

I'd laid it all out. Bracing for his judgment—for him to tell me Thomas was right and that I was selfish—I looked back toward the vista, worried about what I'd see on his face.

Augie was silent for a long time. The only sound was the breeze rustling the trees behind us. When I risked a glance at him, he wasn't looking at me with condemnation. His expression was more like understanding.

"That sounds lonely."

The simple statement wasn't an argument or a critique. It was just a quiet acknowledgment of what I'd done to myself. A lump formed in my throat, and I had to swallow hard against it.

"It is." My voice was barely above a whisper.

"You might think this is crazy, but it reminds me of embroidery, in a way. When I was learning, I kept trying to rush. To get to the finished piece as fast as possible. But my Aunt Rose would say, 'The threads don't care about what you want.' And she was right. If I rushed, I'd tangle everything, make mistakes. Not end up with the result I wanted."

He looked at me, and I managed to meet his gaze. "I think maybe your art and your life are different colors. They don't have to be separate projects. In fact, when you try to keep them apart, you miss the chance to see what they look like woven together."

His words struck me with a force. I thought of the threads in his workroom, the infinite gradients of color bleeding into each other.

"Remember how I said you seemed more easygoing in your directing at the store. After we talked in the park. After you knew me a little better and we had more connection. What if the connection makes the art better, not worse?"

It was a simple question, but it cut to the heart of everything I'd believed about myself. What if Thomas had been right about me, but wrong about the conclusion? What if my problem wasn't that I cared too much about my movie, but that I had believed that I had to be all in on a single thing?

I didn't have an answer. But I was willing to consider the question.

I reached over and took his hand. It was large and engulfed mine completely. He didn't squeeze it or pat it. He just held it. It said more than any words could.

We sat like that for a long time, holding hands under the rich blue sky. The agreement for a no-strings affair seemed even more perilous given the depth of last night and this morning.

For better or worse, I let him see the flawed, messy, unedited footage of my life. How was I supposed to let him go in five days?

THIRTEEN

August

THE DAYS after our trip to the mountain settled into a rhythm. The agreement to embrace the time together had transformed into something deeper than I could've imagined. I'd never connected with someone like I had with Landon. We found an easy flow inside the bubble of his film work, stealing moments between takes, sharing quiet dinners at my house, and falling asleep together.

Landon hadn't surrendered his control completely. On set, he was still the same demanding director, but he was more relaxed while getting the shots he wanted.

He'd let me in. And I managed to let go of some

of the grinding pressure of what Donovan wanted to do to Pine Ridge.

Besides Landon grounding me more, the fact that tourist traffic had picked up markedly helped too. Every day there were more people in town hoping to catch a glimpse of filming, and that was good for every business.

Declan and Brandon were great with the fans clamoring for pictures and autographs. I also got more recognition than I normally did in Pine Ridge as word got around that I was working on the film.

It was a perfect few days. Although I already knew it was going to be tough to say goodbye when the clock ran out in two days.

Landon was also fitting more and more into Pine Ridge, though I doubted he'd admit that. It wasn't a secret we were seeing each other, and everyone had gotten used to us being around town together outside of filming hours.

"You should come with me to the potluck." The idea had been on my mind, and I decided to share it.

"Absolutely not." Landon stood in my kitchen with a dish towel slung over his shoulder. He'd insisted on helping me clean up after dinner, a gesture that made my chest ache with how much I'd miss it. "I already told Felix I wasn't going. I direct chaos for a living, so I don't voluntarily socialize in it."

"It's not chaos." I leaned back against the counter and grinned at him. "It's community. And I'm guessing you already know from Felix that the entire cast and crew are going. It's a thank you from the mayor for the business the film has brought in. If you don't show up, it'll be a thing."

"I'm the director. I am *supposed* to be an antisocial recluse. It's part of my mystique." He scrubbed at a nonexistent spot on a plate with ferocious concentration. "Besides, what do I even bring to a potluck? You already know I don't cook."

I laughed, something I was doing more frequently. "You'd be my guest. And let's not forget, the town's guest. Plus, the movie's caterers are bringing some dishes on behalf of the production, so it's all covered."

Anxiety radiated from him.

"Come on." I closed the distance between us and wrapped my arms around his waist from behind. I rested my chin on his shoulder. His body stiffened for a second before melting back against me. "It'll be fun. You can see one of Pine Ridge's most important traditions. And I'd like to share it with you."

I felt his sigh, a long-suffering sound that I knew was mostly for show. He fought his instincts, the part of him that wanted to keep work and life separate. If he said "no" this time, I'd accept it. I didn't want to risk pushing too hard and spoiling what time we had left.

"Fine," he grumbled, leaning his head back against mine. "But if anyone tries to make me participate in a three-legged race, I'm leaving."

"Deal. I'll protect you from all organized fun."

He turned in my arms, his expression softening, and gave me a slow, lingering kiss that tasted of the wine we'd had with dinner. "You'd better."

***

THE NEXT EVENING WAS WARM, the sun low enough to cast long shadows across the park. Smoke from barbecues drifted through the air, mingling with the scent of fresh bread and the hum of conversation. Pine Ridge residents, film crew, and tourists from the local inns all gathered for what had become the biggest potluck the town had ever seen.

Landon's hand was a warm, nervous presence at the small of my back. It wasn't a possessive gesture, just an anchoring touch. He was stiff, and his eyes scanned the crowd as if he were blocking a scene...or looking for a threat.

"Just relax," I said, my voice low enough for only

him to hear. "These are just people. They don't bite. Mostly."

"Is there a story there about the people who do?" A small smirk played across his face as he relaxed a bit.

The first person who spotted us was Mrs. Miller from the bakery. Her face broke into a wide smile as we came to the dessert table that she'd coordinated.

"Augie! It's good to see you. Isn't it wonderful how many people are here?" Her gaze slid to Landon, her expression curious. "And it's nice to see you here with someone too."

"Mrs. Miller, have you met Landon Winslow? He's the director of the movie."

"We met briefly when he filmed at our place." She wiped her hand on her apron before extending it to him. "It's a pleasure to see you again. Having you and your people in town has been a big help. I never expected so many people to come to watch you all do your work."

"I think that surprised all of us." Landon shook her hand. He was so formal, but his voice was polite and warm. "But I'm glad it's helping the town. Your shop is beautiful, by the way. The shots we've got of the exterior, and looking in the window are fantastic."

"I look forward to seeing it. You just let me know

if you or your people need any pastries," she said, beaming. "It's on the house."

She hugged me before she bustled off toward a group of women who'd come to her table.

As we continued to walk around, I steered Landon through the currents of the crowd. I hadn't expected how much I enjoyed sharing this aspect of Pine Ridge with him.

He was still tense at first, but with each conversation, he became more the version of himself I saw at my house. He endured good-natured grilling from my high school hockey coach about his movie's portrayal of the sport and listened with genuine interest as Mr. Henderson from the hardware store explained the history of the town gazebo. When Shawn and Nick found us, he gave them a wide smile and hugs.

I couldn't stop watching him and how he took it all in. When had he last been part of something like this? He wasn't thinking about framing a scene. He was just... here. Letting the story happen around him instead of trying to control it.

Eventually we got food—a little of everything from the long buffet tables—and found a relatively quiet spot under a large oak tree.

"Doing okay?" I asked as we sat on the ground.

"So far there hasn't been any three-legged racing,

so yes, I'd call it a success." He gave me a brief smile and cocked an eyebrow at me. He took a bite of Mrs. Henderson's potato salad, and his eyes widened. "Oh my God, that's good."

"Told you. Pine Ridge takes its potlucks very seriously. It's a competitive sport."

As we ate, the happy noise of the party was a pleasant buzz around us. A three-piece band set up and played a mix of folk and country that had several couples swaying on a makeshift dance floor. The stars were out, and the lights strung up through the park created a perfect summer night.

"How come you're not eating with us?" Rose plopped on the ground next to us as we were enjoying second helpings of our favorites.

My mind raced to come up with an answer that would satisfy her. "It's nice here under the tree."

She looked suspiciously between us. "He hasn't punched you, has he?" Rose locked eyes on Landon.

"Uh, no." Landon looked my direction. "Were you planning to?"

"You weren't nice in the store the other day." Rose laid it all out.

"Landon, this is my niece, Rose. She can be protective."

A small smile crossed his face. "Just like her uncle."

Thankfully, Paige called for her before we had to answer anything else.

"Be nice to each other." And just like that, she got up and ran off to her mom.

"Sorry about that." I shrugged. "Take a walk with me?"

He nodded, and we got up and set our plates on a table. I led him out of the park and toward town square. As we approached, his expression shifted, his director's eye taking in the way the multi-colored Christmas lights played against the white-painted wood.

"We're shooting the finale tomorrow," he said, his voice thoughtful. "The gazebo scene."

"I know." Taking his hand, I led him up the steps and into the center. "I figured you might want a preview."

The square was empty, everyone else drawn to the food and music. The lights strung along every edge cast a soft, golden glow over everything. I turned to face him, and my breath caught in my throat. He was handsome, with his blue eyes reflecting the twinkling bulbs.

"You seem like you're about to direct me." I couldn't resist teasing him.

He smiled with a smoldering look in his eyes that

sent shudders through me. "I think you've got this one covered."

I took a step closer to him. "The big finale. How does it go again?"

His smile deepened, understanding flashing in his eyes. "Well, Callum finds Julian at the gazebo. He's about to leave town, go back to New York. Callum stops him, tells him that home isn't a place, it's a person."

"Very schmaltzy," I murmured, taking his hands in mine.

"The schmaltziest. But it works because the audience believes it. They want to believe that love can bring two very different people together."

"And do you?" My heart pounded in my chest. "Believe it?"

"I didn't." He spoke so quietly I barely heard him. "Until recently."

Neither of us moved or looked away. Goosebumps formed across my arms as I was drawn in by the openness of his expression.

I pulled out my phone and went to an app that Felix had given me earlier in the day. With the push of a button, the tall evergreen next to the gazebo lit up, exactly as it would be for tomorrow's filming.

Landon gasped as more light flooded the square.

I stepped up to him, caressed his cheek, and

kissed him. We'd kissed plenty over the past few days, but beneath the lights this one was magical. It was full of passion... and love.

Once we came up for air, we were back to looking at each other.

I loved this man.

I couldn't say that out loud, but there was no denying it to my heart.

I swiped at my phone again and triggered the playlist I'd set. A jazzy rendition of "White Christmas" came from the phone's speaker. I held out my hand. "Dance with me."

He looked at me, surprise flickering in his eyes. "Here? Now?"

"Yes."

I set my phone on the bench, and he put his hand in mine without hesitation. I pulled him to me, my arm sliding around his waist, our joined hands to the side.

Gradually, he relaxed against me, his free hand coming up to rest on my shoulder.

We swayed together in the center of the gazebo, surrounded by Christmas decorations in the middle of summer. The music provided a dreamy backdrop as the playlist continued. It was surreal and everything I'd hoped for. The scene would have been perfect for a holiday movie or one of Shawn's books.

After years of casual relationships, I understood what it meant to find your person.

I pulled him close to me, so there was no space between us as we swayed. "We're in a Christmas movie."

He chuckled softly. "We are. A very off-season one."

"I don't know." I tightened my arm around him. "Maybe it's exactly the right season."

He pulled back to look at me, his expression curious. "What do you mean?"

I thought about how to explain the jumble of emotions building in me. Not just having him at the potluck, but watching him really see the town and its people. "Christmas movies are about hope, right? Believing in impossible things. Magic. Connection. Finding home."

"Yes." He placed a kiss on my cheek.

"This summer, I came home fighting for things I thought I might lose. But I found someone I didn't expect. Someone who sees the world differently than I do." I paused, trying to settle my nerves. "You."

His eyes widened as a flush of color rose in his cheeks. He wasn't used to being the main character.

"Augie." He whispered my name.

"I know there are a thousand reasons this can't work." Somehow I kept my voice calm. "You live in

LA. I'm in Denver. You've got *Silo*. I've got the season. But I don't care about any of that. I just care about you."

He was quiet for a long moment, just looking at me. The holiday music swelled, a perfect cinematic cue. Then, he smiled. "I think that's the best dialogue I've heard all summer," he said softly. "Much better than Shawn's gazebo scene."

"Don't tell him that," I laughed.

"I won't." His expression grew serious again. "I'm terrified of how much I want this to work."

"Me too." Relief flooded through me. I hadn't expected him to feel the same way I did. "But maybe that's a good thing. Maybe the scary, unscripted parts are the ones worth fighting for."

He nodded, a small, decisive movement. Then he leaned in, his hand sliding to the back of my neck, and kissed me.

When we pulled apart, I kept him close, our foreheads touching. Around us, the lights twinkled like stars, the fake snow on the ground glittered, and for just a moment, I let myself believe. In magic. In connection. In the impossible idea that a Hollywood director and a Denver hockey player could find a way to be each other's home.

"Let's go... back to my place."

I caught myself before I said "home." I couldn't use that word yet.

His answer was another kiss. "Yes."

The potluck was still in full swing, but people didn't stop us. Instead, we got a lot of smiles and wishes for a "good night" as we passed through the park on the way to my car.

I caught sight of a familiar figure on the periphery. Corbin Donovan, in his usual over-dressed suit, talked with one of the city council. For a moment, the real world with its complications intruded. But, Landon reassuringly squeezed my hand, and I pushed the worries aside to enjoy the time with him.

FOURTEEN

Landon

I WOKE BEFORE DAWN, my mind racing with images and dialogue that demanded to be captured. Augie's bedroom was still dark, the lights along the window providing enough glow to see him sleeping beside me.

Last night at the gazebo had my brain in overdrive. The vulnerability in his eyes as we danced beneath the lights. The way he'd spoken about hope and connection. It was all I could think about.

Carefully, I extricated myself from his embrace. He stirred slightly, a small, discontented sound escaping his lips.

"You okay?" he mumbled.

I leaned down and pressed a kiss to his temple.

"Yeah. I just... I need to write." Memories of Thomas came flooding in, and I worked to push them aside. This was different. "Last night...you... the night... it all clicked."

He blinked up at me, his eyes soft and unfocused. A slow smile spread across his face, and he reached out and took my hand. "Go. Write your masterpiece. I'll see you later."

The simple permission, the unquestioning support, sent a wave of gratitude through me. Thomas would have seen this early-morning departure as a rejection. But Augie understood. He understood the urgency of inspiration, the need to capture it before it evaporated.

I kissed him gently on the lips and dressed in the half-light. Before I left, I paused in the doorway, taking one last look at him. He'd already drifted back to sleep.

Driving along Main Street, the only light I found on was at the bakery as prep was underway for the morning's customers.

As soon as I got to my room, I sat down at the small desk by the window, opened my laptop, and pulled up the *Silo* screenplay. I went to Scene 72— the emotional anchor I'd been struggling to get right for months.

The cursor blinked on the screen, waiting

patiently. But this time, there was no anxiety or fear of failure. Just a certainty about what needed to be written.

I highlighted the three pages of painstakingly crafted, technically proficient, emotionally sterile dialogue.

Delete.

I began to type.

The words didn't come from research or film theory or careful calculation. They came from Augie. The look in his eyes when he'd sat with me in the park after his confrontation with Donovan. His gentle precision working thread through fabric. The confidence he had when he worked with Declan and Brandon on the ice. And then last night.

In the new scene, my farmer John doesn't deliver a speech about the Dust Bowl and economic hardship. He just stands at the window, staring at the horizon. His wife, Sarah, comes to stand beside him. She doesn't ask what's wrong. She stands there, her shoulder pressed against his, a silent, unwavering presence. They stand together for a full page—no dialogue, only the weight of shared burden as they survey their land.

John says one line: "It's all going to go."

And Sarah doesn't promise it will be okay. She doesn't offer a solution. She simply takes his hand.

And he weeps the silent, shoulder-shaking tears of a man who has spent his life carrying the weight of others.

It was stark. It was honest. It was Augie in that park letting me sit with him in the aftermath of Donovan.

I sat back, my fingers hovering above the keyboard. The scene was raw and spare and truthful in a way I'd never managed before.

Thomas used to say I was directing our relationship, of turning him into a supporting character in my own movie. But with Augie, I was experiencing. And somehow, that had made my writing and directing better.

I had been wrong all these years. The choice I had built my entire life around—art or love, never both—was a false dichotomy. Love hadn't weakened my art. It had strengthened it.

I kept writing, and the words flowed freely. The rest of the scene unfolded with a simple economy. No tricks. No artistic flourishes. Just the truth of two people clinging to each other as their world falls apart.

When I finished, it was nearly ten. I'd been writing for hours, lost in a state of flow I hadn't experienced in months. As I read through the scene, I made a few minor adjustments.

It was good. Better than that, it was the best thing I'd ever written.

I called Felix.

"You're calling hours before we're due to start for the day." His voice carried a wariness. "Who died?"

"No one." I couldn't keep the excitement out of my voice. "I rewrote Scene 72."

A pause. "The scene that's been kicking your ass for six months?"

"Yes. And I think I nailed it."

"Send it to me. I'll read it now."

I did, and then paced the room while I waited for his response. Five minutes later, my phone rang.

"Jesus Christ, Lan. This is... I don't even have words."

"It works?"

"Works? It's a fucking masterpiece. Where did this come from?"

I looked out the window at the pine-covered mountains in the distance, at the small town where I'd made Christmas in the middle of summer.

"It came from here. From Augie."

Felix was quiet for a moment. "I'm happy for you, Lan. Not just for the scene. For all of it."

I smiled, grateful for his friendship and not abandoning me even when I was a jerk. "Thanks. I'll see you at the town square in a couple of hours."

THE GAZEBO SCENE was the crown jewel of the movie, the emotional climax that would make or break the entire film. We scheduled it as an eight-hour shoot, with plenty of time for blocking and rehearsals before we started shooting as dusk settled.

When I arrived, the set was already buzzing with activity. Crew members moved with practiced efficiency, setting up lights, checking camera angles, prepping the snow machines. The gazebo and adjacent Christmas tree were a vision of holiday perfection. The fake snow glittered in the afternoon sun.

What surprised me was the crowd. The number of people watching had increased every day. Today, spectators packed in four and five deep behind the barricades around the set. They held up phones, snapping pictures, recording videos. Some had traveled from neighboring states, judging by the license plates on the cars around town.

"Wow, this is a lot. Are we going to have problems with keeping all of them out of the shot?" I asked Felix, who was checking shot lists on his tablet.

"It'll be fine. I worked with the city this morning to get extra barricades up where we need them."

"Do we have that in the budget to manage that

change?" Since we were at the end of the shoot, we didn't have much money to play with.

"They're not charging us. They're thrilled with all the extra people." Felix handed me his phone. "This is what did it. Brandon and Declan were out here this morning and did a post about shooting the movie's final scene today. It went viral quickly, and with all the stuff posted about the shoot already, the internet has decided this is the most adorable Christmas movie ever made. All of these people want to watch live."

I scanned the crowd with a mix of pride and unease. This was good for the movie. Good for the town, too. I noticed several local shops had set up impromptu tables with frozen hot cocoa, snacks, and other merchandise to the visitors.

My gaze landed on a familiar figure standing at the edge of the crowd. Augie was talking to an elderly couple, his head bent to hear them over the noise. He looked relaxed as he gestured toward the gazebo with an animated expression. The man clapped him on the shoulder with obvious affection, and Augie smiled big.

As if sensing my attention, he looked up. Our eyes met across the busy set, and his smile deepened, becoming something more intimate. He excused himself from the couple and made his way toward me.

"Morning... again." He gave me a quick kiss, which flooded me with happiness. "Quite the crowd today."

"The result of a video posted this morning." I was unable to stop smiling. "Your town is becoming famous."

"Apparently. People were talking about it as I came over here." He studied my face, his eyes narrowing slightly. "You seem different."

"Do I?"

"Like you found something you were looking for. The writing went well?"

I thought of the breakthrough that had felt like a dam bursting. "It was... Let me tell you about it later. We've got to get going so we get the lighting right."

A comfortable understanding passed between us. He nodded. "I'll be watching. But don't let me distract you."

"You always distract me." I kept my voice low. "But in the best possible way."

His chuckle sent a wave of contentment through me. He stepped back so he wouldn't be in the way but could see everything.

Felix appeared at my side, a knowing glint in his eye. "Ready to make movie magic?"

I turned to the set with renewed focus. "Let's do it."

The day unfolded with an effortless rhythm I'd rarely experienced on a shoot. Every element seemed to align. The weather held with clear skies and just enough wind to make the fake snow dance in the air. The equipment functioned flawlessly. Even the crowd, which could have been a distraction, provided a perfect energy.

We stayed on schedule too, shooting the lead up in the last moments of the late afternoon. By the time dusk came and the sky was full of color, we were ready for the final declarations and kiss.

The real magic came from the performances.

Despite my earlier frustration—which I knew was more me than them—Declan and Brandon delivered above and beyond so far today.

"Okay, this is it. Places for the finale." Everyone moved into position. "Let's have some snow."

Snow drifted gently around the gazebo where Declan and Brandon stood on their marks.

"Action!" I watched, not on the monitor, but to the scene as it unfolded a few feet away from me.

"Julian, wait," Declan called out as Brandon's character turned to leave.

Brandon paused, his shoulders tense. "Why? Give me one reason to stay in this town."

Declan took a step forward, closing the distance between them. "Because I'm here."

He nailed that line with a vulnerable conviction that gave me chills. This is when the music would swell, a perfect orchestration of strings and piano to underscore the moment.

"What are you saying?" Brandon asked, his voice catching just right.

"I'm saying that home isn't a place. It's a person." Declan's voice pitched perfectly, as if he was telling this to the real love of his life. "And for me... that person is you."

Brandon's reaction felt genuine. He took a hesitant step forward. "But my job... your career..."

"We'll figure it out." Declan reached for Brandon's hand. "Together."

Declan leaned in and kissed Brandon. It was a passionate kiss that captured everything. Brandon added to it by running his hand up Declan's arm to the back of his head, allowing the kiss to deepen.

Behind me, I heard someone weeping. I doubted the mics could pick up that small sound, but even if they had, I wasn't about to stop the scene.

I gave it a few more beats and then called it. "Cut! That was perfect. Absolutely perfect."

The crew and the spectators erupted in spontaneous applause. Declan and Brandon grinned and hugged, clearly feeling the magic of the moment. I caught Felix's eye, and he gave me a subtle thumbs-up. We both knew we'd captured something special.

"Print that," I said, after scanning the playback on the monitor. "But let's do one more, for alternate angles. Also, Declan, instead of holding the kiss, count to about fifteen and then pull back just enough so you two can look lovingly at each other. Okay?"

"Got it. Will do." Declan smiled, and he and Brandon traded a look before they retook starting positions.

As the crew finished up the reset, Augie slid in beside me.

"That was great." His voice was low enough that only I could hear.

"You think?" I asked, curious about his opinion.

"Yeah. I mean, I've watched a lot of these movies, so I know a good ending when I see one. You nailed it."

Coming from Augie, it was the highest praise possible. I felt a ridiculous surge of pride.

"That was amazing." Felix joined us at the monitor. "I haven't seen you this relaxed directing since the Bauer commercial."

The Bauer commercial had won me my first industry award. It had been the beginning of my career, when I was still driven by pure passion rather than ambition.

"Maybe I found my way back to something," I said.

Felix smiled and looked between me and Augie. "Maybe you did."

We got one more perfect take before the sky settled into dark for the night.

"That's a wrap on the gazebo and town square!" I announced.

Felix clapped me on the back, his face split in a wide grin. "That's the money shot, Lan. Ted is going to love it."

I felt a surge of professional pride. I had delivered and proven I could do this. My path to *Silo* was clear.

With shooting completed, Declan and Brandon were posing for selfies with fans at the barricade, their charm on full display. I spotted Augie talking to a group of teenagers, signing something for one of them.

"We've been selling out of everything." Mrs. Miller approached with a tray of cinnamon rolls. She offered them to the crew, and I happily took one because I knew how good they were. "I had to call my niece to come help. It's literally like Christmas!"

"Glad to hear it." I wondered how much all of this would be able to help fend off Donovan.

"Oh, it's been a godsend. I told Augie this morning that if he'd known his hockey money couldn't save his family store and Main Street, he should have just brought a movie to town years ago!" She chuckled, but I didn't find it funny.

"His hockey money?"

"Oh, he's been helping keep Reeve's Textiles afloat for years. Between the quiet winters and that online competition... well, it's been tight for everyone. But he wants to take the store over when he retires, so he's a financial lifeline when he needs to be."

She moved on to offer pastries to more of the crew, leaving me with a new piece of the puzzle. Augie hadn't just been fighting for his family's legacy —he'd been subsidizing it. The weight he carried was even heavier than I'd realized.

But as I looked around the triumphant set, Augie wasn't where he had been a moment before. Instead, he stood apart from the crowd, his attention fixed on something down the street. His posture had changed, the easy calm from earlier gone.

I followed his line of sight and saw a man in a suit moving from shop to shop along Main Street.

But it wasn't Donovan. At each business, he handed over an envelope.

"Augie?" I called, making my way toward him.

He didn't look at me, his eyes still fixed on what was happening. "I need to check on something. I'll catch up with you later."

Before I could respond, he was moving down the street, his pace quickening with each step. The man arrived at Reeve's Textiles before Augie did. I was too far away to see what was happening.

"Everything okay?" Felix asked, clapping my shoulder.

"I don't think so." Anxiety settled in my stomach.

Felix followed my gaze to the textile store. The man with the envelopes left and headed up the block to the next business.

"I'm sure Augie will take care of it," Felix said, but his voice lacked conviction. "Come on, we need to check these shots to make sure we don't have anything from here to add to the pickup list for tomorrow."

I allowed myself to be led back to the monitor, but my mind was no longer on the perfect scene we'd captured. My focus stayed on Augie and the sudden tension in his shoulders as he entered the store.

FIFTEEN

August

I ARRIVED at the store just as the man was leaving. Through the glass, I saw Paige standing frozen behind the counter, a thick cream-colored envelope in her hands, her expression unreadable.

The bell chimed as I pushed through the door.

"Paige?"

She looked up, her eyes finding mine. She didn't speak, just handed me the papers she'd been reading. The first thing I noticed was the heavy, expensive stock with "Donovan Development" embossed in the corner.

"Is it what I think it is?"

She nodded, running a hand through her hair. "Read it."

The opening paragraph was enough:

Final Notice: Pursuant to Washington State Code Section 8.12.030 and Pine Ridge Municipal Ordinance 47.6, Donovan Development Inc. hereby gives final notice of the proposed acquisition of the property at 142 Main Street, operating as Reeve's Textiles,' for the purpose of a significant public works project as defined under state law...

"What is this?" I could barely speak through the anger building in my chest. "What's he trying to pull now?"

Paige leaned against the counter and gave a look toward the back of the store. We weren't alone. Paige kept the store open late, like most of the businesses, to take advantage of the film crowd.

"It's called eminent domain, Augie," she said, keeping her voice down. "If we don't take this offer and the council votes that Donovan's development constitutes 'significant public benefit' in terms of jobs, tax revenue, and tourism, they can legally force us to sell. Market value, no negotiation."

I stared at her, the words not fully registering. "They can't do that. This is our property. It's been in the family for..."

"A hundred years. I know." She took the letter back from me, folding it with precise, angry creases.

"But it turns out a century of history doesn't mean much against the right legal maneuvers."

I felt like I'd taken a blindside hit on the ice, the kind that leaves you laid out and gasping. "When is this supposed to happen?"

"The vote is in three weeks." She tapped the second page. "Mark Halliday, one of two holdouts on the council, came by earlier. He said three other members are ready to approve the deal. Apparently, Donovan's been leaning on them hard."

Three weeks. An execution date for everything my family had built.

"This isn't over." I tried to sound confident even though the ground beneath my conviction was far from stable. "They haven't voted yet. We can fight this."

My first instinct was to call Landon. He'd understand the weight of this.

"Donovan's made his final offer to everyone." Paige interrupted my thoughts. "Clara and Frank Miller are considering it."

That hit like another body check.

"I should go talk to Mrs. Miller." I headed toward the door.

"Augie." Paige's voice stopped me. "This isn't just about the money anymore. Donovan's being strategic. He told the Millers he'd buy all their equipment at full value and keep Clara on as manager of the new *artisan patisserie* he's planning. With Frank's health issues, they need the medical insurance."

The implication was clear. Donovan wasn't just buying buildings. He was buying futures. Security. An easy way out of the struggle.

I found Clara Miller in the back of the bakery, kneading dough with the same intense concentration I'd seen since I was a kid. The muscles in her forearms worked rhythmically, a lifetime of craft in every movement.

She looked up when I entered, never stopping her work. Her eyes were tired, but her smile was genuine. "Augie. I was wondering when you'd stop by."

"You got one too," I said, not bothering with pleasantries.

She nodded, her gaze returning to the dough. "We did."

"Are you considering it?"

Her hands stilled for just a moment before resuming their steady work. "We don't want to, but..." Her tone was soft, apologetic. "Frank needs a double knee replacement. The specialist isn't covered by our insurance. The offer Donovan's making would pay for that and then some."

"We can figure something out." Desperation edging into my voice. "The town could hold a fundraiser, or I could—"

"It's not just the surgery." She sighed, wiping her hands on her apron. "It's everything. The building needs a new roof. The industrial mixer is on its last legs. We're barely breaking even most months. And our kids don't want the business." She looked at me, her eyes suddenly fierce. "I'm sixty-three, August. I've been standing on this same concrete floor since I was fifteen. I'm tired."

The defeat in her voice made me sad. The Millers were part of Pine Ridge's history, part of its heart. If she was ready to give up...

"I want to stand with you." Her words were quieter, weighted with resignation. "My family's been here as long as yours. I'm just not sure we can anymore. As much as we'd hoped the movie could fix things, Donovan's not giving that a chance to be true."

I nodded, but couldn't speak. What could I say?

"I understand." There was no way to keep the defeat out of my tone.

She came around the counter and hugged me. She smelled of cinnamon and yeast, a scent that took me back to childhood. "We haven't made a final decision yet. But I needed you to know where things stand."

I returned her embrace, and we just held each other for a moment. We agreed to check in with each other tomorrow.

The sidewalk outside was still bustling with activity as the film crew packed up from the shoot and the spectators milled around. I spotted Shawn, his face animated as he talked with a production assistant. In another life—the one I'd been living less than an hour ago—I might have gone to join him.

Instead, I turned and walked in the opposite direction, needing space. My feet carried me to the park and the bench by the pond.

The reality of the situation crystallized with brutal clarity. This was never just about Reeve's Textiles. It was about the Millers and their medical needs. It was about Mr. Henderson at the hardware store, whose son started college next year. It was all about the small vulnerabilities that Donovan had identified and now exploited.

My phone buzzed in my pocket.

Landon: *Are you okay?*

My thumb hovered over the message.

Coach Brennan's words echoed in my head: "You're not alone on the ice, Reeve." It was a lesson he'd tried to drum into me after I'd played through a hairline fracture in my wrist during a crucial playoff game my junior year of high school. I hadn't told anyone about the injury until after we'd won.

"The team isn't just there for the glory," he'd said. "They're there for the pain too. That's what makes a team into a unit, not just a collection of guys in the same jerseys."

But this wasn't the ice. This wasn't a game with clear rules and defined endpoints. This was my family's legacy, the town I cared about. It wasn't Landon's problem. It was mine.

Landon had *Silo*. His passion project. His future waited for him in LA. His life was finally coming together. This wasn't his burden to bear.

I slipped the phone back into my pocket without replying. The silence of the park enveloped me, broken only by the occasional call of a bird and leaves rustling in the breeze.

"There you are."

I looked up to find Landon standing on the path, his expression a mixture of relief and concern.

"Hey," I said, my voice rough with emotion.

He came and sat beside me. "I was looking for you." He studied my face, his gaze sharp and perceptive. "What's happened?"

"Nothing," I said automatically.

"August." The way he said my name—not Augie, but my full name—was gentle but firm. "I know you. And I know something's happened. Everyone saw the guy delivering envelopes."

I looked at him, at the genuine concern in his eyes, and conflicting emotions collided in my brain. Gratitude for his perception. Guilt for my instinct to shut him out. Fear that sharing this would only make it more real.

"It's complicated."

"I've got time." He reached out and took my hand.

The wall of isolation I'd been trying to erect crumbled before I could even finish building it. I took a deep breath and told him everything.

His expression grew serious as I spoke. When I finished, he was quiet for a long moment, his thumb caressing the back of my hand.

"Three weeks," he said finally. "That's not much time, but it's something. We can work with that."

The "we" caught me off guard. A small, selfish part of me couldn't help but be gratified by how quickly he made my fight into *our* fight. The larger, more protective part felt the guilt. His production here was wrapping, but he had more to do in L.A.

"Landon, you don't have to—"

"Don't." He cut me off gently. "Don't do that

thing where you try to handle everything alone." He squeezed my hand. "I'm here. I want to help. Let me help."

His sincerity was almost painful to witness. I looked away, my gaze fixing on the still surface of the pond. "I don't think there's anything to be done." It hurt to say that. "If the council votes for it... that's it. Game over."

"Then we change the game." A familiar spark of creative energy lit up his eyes. He didn't release me, but his free hand gestured in the air as it did when he was blocking a scene. "This is a story, right? It's a classic David versus Goliath narrative. Small, family-owned businesses against a soulless corporate developer. People love that kind of story. Hell, they make Christmas movies about it every year."

I recognized the shift in him as he went from empathetic listener to problem-solver.

"So, we have to get the story out there." He talked faster as the ideas came to him. "We need a publicity campaign. We've already got a solid base, thanks to all the buzz from the shoot. Plus, there's the human-interest angle. Felix and I have contacts at a few of the big LA papers, the kind that have national reach. We could pitch them. 'NHL Star Fights to Save Hometown Legacy.' It's a great headline."

A knot formed in my stomach. He was so sure, so

confident in his Hollywood solutions. As if a well-placed article could stop the inexorable legal machinery that was already in motion.

"And we need a social media element." His eyes sparkled with creative energy. "We create a hashtag. #SavePineRidge, or #ReevesForever, something catchy. We can get Shawn and Nick to post about it. Declan and Brandon have millions of followers between them. They can do a video from Main Street. It can become a national cause. Just the negative publicity alone might make Donovan back off."

He looked at me with a triumphant expression. He had found the narrative and rewritten the third act.

And I felt nothing but a profound, soul-crushing exhaustion.

"You don't get it, Landon." My voice cracked with emotion.

His smile faltered. "What do you mean? It's a solid plan. It reframes the narrative—"

"This isn't a narrative," I interrupted. "You can't reframe this. This is my life. Paige's life. The Millers'. It's not something you can fix with a hashtag."

"I'm not trying to fix it with a hashtag," he said, no longer sounding excited. Another surge of guilt hit me for deflating his enthusiasm. "I'm trying to use the tools I have to help. These things work. Public pressure can change things."

"Can it change a town council vote that's already been bought and paid for?" Bitterness rose in my throat. "Can it stop a developer from using a legal loophole to seize an entire street of businesses? The fight's over, Landon."

I watched the confident, creative fire in his eyes die out, replaced by a look of stunned, helpless confusion.

"I... I don't know what that means." He looked completely lost.

"Of course you don't." I couldn't stop the harshness of my words. "It means the town can just take our land for *public benefit*. It's a checkmate. There's no appeal. There's no grand gesture that can stop it. It's just... the end."

I stood up, my body feeling heavy.

"I'm sorry," he whispered as he got up. "Augie, I'm so sorry."

His sympathy was the last thing I wanted. I needed to get away from him. Away from his well-meaning, hopeful optimism that only highlighted the depth of my failure.

I looked him in the eye, and the man I saw was a stranger. A handsome, talented stranger from a world of make-believe. I should've never suggested that we be more than co-workers.

"It's not yours to worry about. It's not your problem. This is my life. This is my town's life. And you are not a part of it."

I didn't wait for his response. I couldn't watch the hurt on his face—it would only add to my sadness.

SIXTEEN

Landon

THE COLOR-CODED schedule on my trailer wall seemed to mock me with its pristine, perfect order. A precise grid of index cards and push pins that represented fourteen days of meticulous planning, culminating in today—*Day 14: Final Shots. Main Street.*

Every day I'd spent in Pine Ridge was there, neatly categorized.

Except for the one thing I hadn't planned for, and couldn't control. August... Augie.

I woke alone in my bed at the B&B. I hadn't spent the night here in days. For a moment, I reached across the empty sheets, seeking a warmth that wasn't there.

My phone screen had no texts or missed calls from the person I most wanted to hear from. Instead it was full of production notifications from Felix and a weather report promising another perfect day. I dropped the device back on the nightstand.

I showered, dressed in my usual black jeans and t-shirt, and moved through the morning routine. Coffee. Schedule check. Shot list review. The movements of a director preparing for his day. It was a role that, thankfully, I could play on autopilot.

I'd need it for today since sleep had been elusive. Every time I closed my eyes, I saw him walking away in the park, his broad shoulders slumped with hurt.

It's not your problem. This is my life. This is my town's life. And you are not a part of it.

He'd been right. His fight with the developer and the threat to his home weren't narrative problems to be fixed. They were real, complicated issues with real stakes. I'd offered him Hollywood solutions, treating his life like a script that needed punching up.

No wonder he'd walked away.

I arrived on set as the crew set up along Main Street, cables snaking across the sidewalk, lights being positioned to catch the warm morning glow on the storefronts. At the end of the block, the gazebo stood bare. It was just another wooden structure in a small town.

"Morning, boss." Felix appeared at my side, tablet in hand, the same way he'd done every day of this shoot. "We're set for the insert shots. The cookie plate and steaming cocoa mug at Mrs. Miller's are ready. Brandon's in makeup for the reaction shot at the post office. Declan's headed into wardrobe so he can join Brandon for the shots we need up and down Main Street. We should be wrapped by three if everything goes to plan."

"Good." I trusted what Felix said was correct. I was busy scanning the street, a reflex I couldn't stop. Looking for him.

Felix followed my gaze. "You okay?"

"I'm fine." I took the tablet from his hands, scrolling through the day's call sheet with unnecessary intensity. "Let's get the cookie plate and hot chocolate first. I want to catch the natural light through the bakery's front window."

Felix didn't push. He knew me well enough to recognize I had nothing more to say. "Right. We'll be ready within fifteen."

I moved through the morning in a fog of professional focus, calling out camera positions, checking angles, giving terse approvals. "Good." "Fine." "Let's move on." I was just running out the clock until I could retreat to LA.

"Can we get more back light on that steam?" I called out, watching as a production assistant adjusted the angle of a small LED panel illuminating the rising vapor from a mug of cocoa. "It's not reading on camera. And pull the cookie with the chip sticking up. It's creating a conflicting focal point."

This was the kind of obsessive control that once would have brought me satisfaction. But having lived a different reality the past few days, it wasn't how I wanted to be. Unfortunately, it was also the only way I'd get through the day because otherwise I'd dwell on what I'd lost.

Around noon, as we set up Brandon's reaction shot outside the post office, I spotted him.

Augie was across the street, talking to Mr. Henderson. Even from a distance, I clocked the tension in his shoulders and how he gestured with his hands as he made a point. My heart ached knowing the pain he was in and not being able to help.

"Landon?" Felix's voice brought me back. "We're ready."

I tore my gaze away and stepped to the monitor.

Augie continued his conversation, seemingly oblivious to my existence.

The afternoon dragged on. We moved down our shot list, collecting the final pieces of the puzzle that the editor and I would assemble in post-production. A warm, comforting Christmas movie that would stream into millions of homes, viewers unaware of the real story that had unfolded behind the scenes.

At two forty-five, we set up for the final sequence of several shots with Declan and Brandon walking up and down Main Street in different outfits and different combinations of people. Felix had even invited some of the tourists who'd stuck around for several days to appear in the final shots as extras—a small thank-you for their support.

I stared at the monitor, at the cheerful, festive image, and felt nothing. No satisfaction. No relief. Just a desire to reshoot the ending I'd had with Augie.

"Ready for the final call, boss?" Felix asked.

I waited a beat, watching the perfect, meaningless image on the screen. "And... action."

The camera panned, following Declan as he walked past five storefronts. The shot lasted less than thirty seconds.

"Cut," I said.

A beat of silence. Then Felix's voice, loud and clear and full of genuine joy, rang out across Main Street. "That is a picture wrap on *Christmas in the Cascades!*"

Cheers, whistles, and applause came from every direction. Crew members hugged, slapped each other on the back. Someone popped a bottle of champagne. A crowd of tourists and locals who'd been watching joined in the celebration, phones raised to capture the moment.

Felix enveloped me in a fierce, backslapping hug. "You did it! You actually did it! On time! On budget! Ted called while you were setting up the last shot. He's over the moon having seen the footage from yesterday. *Silo* is a go, Lan. He's sending you the paperwork in the next few days."

I managed a smile. I felt like an actor who wasn't quite ready for their big scene. "It was a team effort."

Felix pressed a plastic flute of champagne into my hand. "Most of it was you bringing it all together. The dailies are incredible. Ted says it's some of the best holiday footage he's seen." He lowered his voice, his expression serious. "And the scenes you rewrote for *Silo?* He called them 'a revelation.' You did it, Lan. You got everything you wanted."

Everything I wanted. That wasn't true.

I couldn't have what I actually needed.

My phone buzzed in my pocket. A text from Ted

himself: "You delivered. Consider *Silo* greenlit. Full funding. Your passion project is a go."

It was the call I had been waiting for my entire professional life. The culmination of years of compromise, of directing commercials for products I hated and episodic television I didn't respect.

I thanked him via text, my fingers moving on instinct. After I hit send, I just stared at the screen for a long time. It was meaningless since I couldn't share it with Augie, the person responsible for my breakthrough.

Scanning the faces of the celebrating crowd, I found Augie near the edge of the gathering. He wasn't celebrating. He stood with his sister, watching the scene. As I stared, he glanced my way, our eyes meeting. I couldn't read his expression. Suddenly he turned, said something to Paige, and walked away, disappearing down a side street.

As the afternoon wore on, the celebration migrated from Main Street to The Keg Saloon. The cast and crew packed into the bar along with many locals and tourists. Music blared from the jukebox, and rounds of shots passed through the crowd.

Everyone wanted to say something to me. There were toasts. There were congratulations. There were people asking to stay in touch for future projects. More selfies were taken.

I smiled, nodded, and accepted their praise. I did my best to hide the misery I felt.

"Smile any harder and your face might crack." Felix appeared beside me at the bar and handed me a whiskey. It reminded me of the first drink I'd had at Augie's house. "You look like you're at a funeral, not a wrap party."

I took a long swallow, welcoming the burn. "Just tired."

"Bullshit," he countered gently. "I've seen you tired. Sleep-deprived, stressed, angry. Hell, I've seen you direct for thirty-six hours straight when you had to. This isn't tired. This is..." He searched my face. "He's not here."

The statement only confirmed what I knew.

"His job is done," I said, my voice carefully neutral. I took another sip of whiskey.

"His job's been done for days," Felix pointed out. "Didn't stop him from exercising his contractual right to be on set to watch."

I didn't have an answer for that. I just stared into my glass. We stood in companionable silence for a few minutes, the joyous chaos of the party swirling around our small, quiet island.

"We're trending, by the way." Felix pulled out his phone and showed me a social media feed where #ChristmasInTheCascades was climbing. There were posts from Declan, Brandon, crew members, and all the spectators we had. There are already tens of thousands of likes. "The publicity team wants to drop the trailer within the next two weeks. They want to capitalize on the behind-the-scenes footage."

I nodded absently. The thought of the movie's release, coming just a few months after Donovan's win, seemed like a bitter blow for everyone who lived here.

Felix's expression softened. "Go find him, Lan."

"What?"

"Go. Find. Him." Felix took the glass from my hand. "This isn't going anywhere." He gestured around at the bar. "But he might be."

I looked at him and saw the genuine concern in his eyes. Felix had been with me through every professional high and low. He saw me and Thomas fall apart. He'd never once suggested I walk away from a production celebration.

But before I could respond, the front door of the saloon opened, letting in a slice of the early evening air.

It was him.

Augie stood just inside the doorway, framed against the dark street. His hair was damp, as if he'd recently showered. He wore a simple gray T-shirt and jeans. His gaze swept the room.

Our eyes met, and the world snapped into sharp focus. The anger vanished from his face. The stony expression he'd worn on the street earlier slipped away, too. All that remained was what appeared to be grief.

"I have to go."

Felix nodded, his expression full of sad understanding. "Yes, you do."

I pushed my way through the crowd. "Landon, another drink!" "Hey, Winslow, come over here!" The voices didn't matter. I needed to get to the man by the door who looked like his world had ended.

When I reached him, I didn't know what to say.

"Hey." His voice was barely audible over the music.

"Hey."

We stood there for a moment, looking at each other.

"Can we...?" I started, not knowing how to finish the sentence. Go? Talk? Pretend?

He gave a single nod. He turned and pushed the door open, and I followed him out to the quiet street. We walked down Main Street. The Christmas decorations were gone, already stripped away by the crew. The town was back to how it should look in late July.

We stayed quiet for a long time. I wasn't sure if

that was good or bad. It alternated between comfort-able and needing to be filled.

When we got to my B&B, we stopped at the bottom of the porch steps. The lights inside, creating a welcoming glow.

He didn't look at me but instead focused on the front door of the inn. "So this is it," he said, his voice void of all emotion. "You leave tomorrow?"

"Afternoon flight," I confirmed.

He nodded again. "Me too. I guess I'll say goodbye here."

He turned to go.

He planned to say goodnight and walk away? Our final scene would be a quiet, anticlimactic goodbye on a sidewalk.

The storyteller in me screamed that it was the wrong ending.

I gripped his hand so he couldn't leave. He didn't even glance my way. "Don't go," I whispered. "Not yet."

He was still for a long, agonizing moment. A slight tremor went through him before he turned to me. He looked exhausted. "What's the point?"

"I just... I don't want it to be over yet."

He sighed. "I don't either."

He let me lead him up the steps and into my

room. The space was neat, with my suitcase already half-packed in the corner.

There was no talk. There were no grand pronouncements of love or regret.

I stepped closer, and he wrapped his arms around my waist. Burying my face in his neck, I breathed in the familiar scent of him.

Our mouths met slow, tender, and desperate. He returned every kiss, and I knew he wanted this as much as I did.

Guiding him toward the bed, we undressed each other. I wanted to commit each of his touches to memory, tracing the familiar lines of his body—the broad, strong shoulders, the hard planes of his stomach.

We were two people who cared for each other, making one last connection. We alternated between hungry passion and more relaxed moves to make this last as long as possible. My climax was a silent, shuddering release. Augie followed a moment later, his body going rigid in my arms with a single, broken moan.

Afterward, I held him close, his back pressed against my chest. I felt the moment exhaustion claimed him and he finally relaxed as he drifted to sleep.

But sleep wouldn't come for me. I lay there in the

dark, feeling his steady, rhythmic breathing. The celebration at The Keg felt like it had happened a lifetime ago. All that mattered was the man in my arms. This impossible, stubborn, beautiful man who had crashed into my life and made my art better. He'd also made me feel a connection that I didn't think was possible for me.

After tomorrow, I'd probably never see him again.

SEVENTEEN

August

As soon as I woke up, the anxiety inflicted by Donovan's letter overtook my thoughts. When I finally opened my eyes, I was also in an unfamiliar place.

It took a moment for the memories of last night to kick in. Landon's room at the B&B came into focus with the white sheets, his back rising and falling in slow rhythm, and his tousled dark hair against the pillow.

Sliding carefully out of bed, I crossed to the window and looked out to where the first hint of dawn colored the sky. Vermont waited with a hockey camp full of young players. In any other summer, I'd be looking forward to working with them. But the thought of leaving Pine Ridge, and of leaving Landon, made enthusiasm impossible.

I found my jeans and t-shirt from yesterday, discarded on a chair, and pulled them on. Behind me, I heard the rustle of sheets.

"Augie?" Landon sounded sleepy, and his use of my nickname stabbed my heart.

"I'm here." I returned my focus to looking outside.

The bed creaking signaled his movement. The silence stretched, filled with the things we couldn't say.

"It's early," he said finally.

"We do have a long drive to Seattle." I turned to face him. "Your car's still at The Keg. I need to grab my bags from my place. Unless you think it'd be better..."

He shook his head. "No. I want as much time with you as I can have."

There was no holding back a smile, even as I suspected the drive might only make the final goodbye more difficult.

I watched as he rose, his movements economical and controlled as he gathered his clothes and set about packing the rest of his things.

On the small desk by the window, I noticed the screenplay for *Silo* printed out. Handwritten notes filled the margins in Landon's neat script. Curiosity tugged at me, but it felt wrong to ask if I could read it.

"I'm going to head to my place and get my stuff together. I'll be ready when you get there."

"Sounds good. I'll grab a quick shower and then get going. Should be there within the half hour. That work?" Landon looked like he wanted to say more.

"Yeah. See you then."

Neither of us moved for a moment, but I kicked myself into motion. I gave him a single nod and left the room.

***

I STOOD on the porch of my house, my hockey bag and luggage at my feet, waiting for Landon.

After I got packed, I'd stopped in my workroom and looked over the in-progress project in the embroidery hoop. The town square, transformed by Landon's movie, captured in tiny stitches. It was just about half-finished, the gazebo and tree complete, but there were still a lot of pencil marks on fabric waiting to be filled in.

After yesterday, I wasn't sure I'd finish it. Somehow, leaving it unfinished felt right under the circumstances.

Landon's rental car pulled up. He stayed behind the wheel and watched me as I moved toward the car. I loaded my bags in next to his, filling the trunk with our possessions. More than anything, I wanted to go somewhere with him rather than separating at the airport.

I slid into the passenger seat, the console ensuring that a few inches remained between us.

Landon didn't turn on the radio. The only sounds were the hum of the engine and the whoosh of the tires on the highway. The familiar landscape of the Cascades was usually a source of comfort, but now even the towering firs and misty peaks seemed anything but. Instead, it felt like it was all chastising me, "You failed. You let this go."

"What's next for the movie?" I asked, unable to maintain silence but also wanting some neutral ground. "When will it be finished?"

Landon shifted in his seat, his body language easing with the professional topic I'd offered. "Post-production takes about six weeks. Editing, sound mixing, color correction, score integration..." He listed the technical steps like he was reading from a manual, his voice taking on the precision I recognized from set.

"Are you involved in all of that?"

"I'll be working with the editor. Some of the

other areas I'll sign off on. The first thing we have to do is get the trailer done. The studio loves the footage, as well as the internet buzz the film has from all the behind the scenes and spectator posts. They want to... to... uhm... capitalize on all of that."

Guilt joined the anxiety I already had going. Landon had mentioned trying to use social media against Donovan. Maybe I should've listened to his idea rather than shutting it down.

It was time for a topic change. "You never told me how your writing session went," I said after a long pause. "For *Silo*. That morning..." I didn't finish the sentence.

Landon's grip tightened on the steering wheel. "It was a breakthrough, actually." Despite the tension in his hands, he sounded enthusiastic. "I rewrote the scene I'd been stuck on for months."

"That's great." A surge of happiness washed over me, pushing other concerns away for a moment.

"It was because of you." The words hung between us, an admission neither of us knew what to do with. "Between my revisions and how *Christmas in the Cascades* came together, I got official notice that the film is funded. The contracts should be signed any day now."

The urge to touch him was difficult to stop, but I couldn't let myself do it because I might not let go.

"I... That's the best news. Congratulations." I pulled my hand back and dropped it to my side.

"Thanks." He looked over and smiled as his hands relaxed on the wheel.

We fell silent again for a few miles.

"Are you looking forward to the hockey camp?" Landon kept his tone deliberately light.

"The timing is terrible, but yeah, I am." He winced at my mention of timing. "Ten days working with teenagers with a range of skills. I coach power skating and shooting technique, with a mix of tactical work too. It's always a great time." I spoke with more animation, the coach in me overshadowing the heartbreak. "There are a few good college prospects in the mix for the session too."

"You enjoy teaching." It wasn't a question. He'd seen me with the local kids at the rink.

"I do. It's a good way to give back. And a friend of mine runs the camp, so I'm happy to be there for a couple of weeks." I glanced out the window, watching the familiar landmarks of the route to Seattle tick by too quickly. "After that, I'll be back in Pine Ridge with just a few days before the vote about Main Street happens. And then it's only a couple more weeks before I'm back in Denver."

I thought of Nick and Shawn, making their long-distance relationship work despite their schedules.

For a moment, I let myself imagine a similar arrangement with Landon.

But the Mountaineers had 41 away games, and an equal number of home games to play. And Landon had to finish *Christmas in the Cascades* and start work on *Silo*. Our lives were separated in so many ways, it felt like we'd always be playing on different teams with no chance of a trade.

There wasn't much more to discuss. The small talk between us was almost painful. It was still better than the silence, where there was no avoiding the fact that we both had things to say that we weren't.

As we arrived at SeaTac, Landon followed the signs for Departures. The impersonal world of the airport enveloped us. The concrete structures and color-coded airline directions.

He pulled up to the curb in front of my terminal. He put the car in park, but he didn't turn off the engine.

"Well," I said with a sigh, "I guess this is it."

He just nodded, his gaze fixed somewhere beyond the windshield.

All around us, other goodbyes happened—families hugging, couples kissing, tearful embraces that would be followed by reunions in days or weeks. Normal separations. Temporary ones. Not the final one we were making.

"Your flight is at 2:15?" Landon asked, checking his watch. All business. All logistics.

"Yeah. Yours is at 4:30, right?"

"Yes."

What if we tried...? The words formed in my mind, but I couldn't say them. "Do you have everything?" I asked instead, falling back on the practical tasks.

He nodded again, a short, efficient movement. "I do."

I unbuckled my seatbelt, opened the door and stepped onto the sidewalk.

Landon got out, too. He came around the car and stood on the bustling sidewalk while I pulled my bags from the trunk. He had his hands shoved in his pockets, his shoulders hunched.

I searched for the right words and wondered if he was doing the same.

"Have a good time at camp." He had a formal tone, which I wasn't used to hearing. "And a great season, August."

He said my full name. It was another signal. A return to the beginning, before *Augie* and the feelings we'd developed.

"You too," I said, my voice just as stilted. "I can't wait to see the movie. And good luck with *Silo*."

The silence that followed was excruciating. This

was the moment for a final gesture. A handshake. A hug. Something. But we stood frozen, our hands at our sides. My fingers twitched, wanting to reach for him, to touch him one last time.

He gave me a small nod.

He turned, walked back to the car, and drove away without a backward glance. I stood on the curb, my bags next to me, and watched the taillights of his rental car disappear into the chaotic traffic.

He was gone.

I had to move. I had a flight to catch. A life to lead.

Grabbing my bags, I went through the sliding glass doors and into the terminal. The chaos of the airport was easy to lose myself in. My sole focus was supposed to be on camp, not Landon or the problems I'd left at home.

After I checked my hockey bag and got through security, I found directions for my gate and started the long walk. I kept my eyes fixed on the signs ahead.

My phone buzzed in my pocket. I pulled it to read the text as I walked.

Ethan: *Looking forward to having you here! I just sent you details about the campers for the session. It's going to be a fun one. Hope you have a good flight. I know you're getting in late, so I'll see you for breakfast in the morning. Text me or Liam if you need anything in the meantime.*

The words pulled me toward the future, toward camp, and toward another season. I'd be working with talented young players. I'd be returning to a team that I loved playing for and a city where I had friends and a life. It was a good life. It was the life I'd chosen over staying in Pine Ridge. On any other day, Ethan's text would have sparked excitement.

A wild, reckless thought seized me. I could buy a ticket to LA. I could follow Landon and show up at his door. Tell him I'd made a terrible mistake.

Reality caught up fast, reminding me of my responsibilities—to the camp, my team, and home, whatever was left of it after Donovan.

As I arrived at the gate, boarding had already begun. Once I got myself situated in my seat, I closed my eyes, hoping I'd find the right mental energy by the time I arrived in Vermont.

EIGHTEEN

Landon

My world was made up of the rectangle screens on the monitors in a dark editing bay. I had been staring at the same sequence for hours, trying to get the sequence in Reeve's Textiles perfect. I owed that to August.

It was almost midnight. The rest of the post-production team had gone home hours ago, leaving me alone with the ghosts of Pine Ridge. I rubbed my eyes, feeling the rough scrape of stubble on my face. When had I last shaved? The days had blurred together since I'd returned to Los Angeles.

It'd been nearly two weeks of eighteen-hour workdays. I slept on the leather couch in my office—

if I slept at all. Food consisted of black coffee and whatever Felix forced into my hands.

On screen, the image froze on the interior of Reeve's Textiles. The bolts of fabric arranged just so. The counter where August and Paige worked as background extras. I couldn't escape him. He was everywhere. Even if he wasn't on screen, I remembered where he stood on the set for every scene.

I'd be in a color-timing session, trying to get the nostalgic glow of the textile shop right, and all I could see was him, standing belligerently by the quilt rack during our first meeting. The editor would ask if I liked the saturation, and I would have to swallow the lump in my throat before I answered.

I'd be in the sound mix, listening to the foley artist layer in the crisp, scraping sound of skates on ice, and I was right back on the rink, watching him move. Not Declan on screen, but August working with Declan on his skating.

The worst was the final gazebo scene. We had to watch it over and over, tweaking the music, adjusting the atmospheric sound, making sure the fake snow looked right. Every time Declan delivered the line about home being a person, a wave of self-loathing so potent it was nauseating would wash over me.

I'd found a home in a person.

And I'd let it slip away.

A soft knock on the editing bay door startled me. I hadn't even heard it open.

Felix stood in the doorway, holding two cups of coffee from the 24-hour place down the street. He looked tired, but his eyes were sharp, missing nothing.

"You look like shit." He walked in and set one of the coffees on the console next to me.

"I'm working." I kept my focus on the monitor in front of me.

"So I see." He pulled up a rolling chair and slumped into it with a sigh. "When was the last time you left this building? I think it's been at least five days. Even for you, that's a bit much. I'm pretty sure the union has rules about this. Something about cruel and unusual punishment."

I took a sip of the coffee. It was hot and bitter, exactly what I needed. "Just want to get it done."

"It is done, Lan. Everything that's left for the rough cut you could leave to the team and review it before it goes to Ted." He gestured around the dark, cold room. "You don't have to be here."

"I want to be here." I shot him a defiant look.

Felix was silent, studying me. "Okay, this has gone on long enough."

"I don't know what you're talking about."

"Bullshit." The word was quiet but firm. "I'm

your producer who manages your budgets, your schedules, and even the studio heads. But I'm also your friend. And as your friend, I'm telling you that you're a wreck. This is supposed to be your victory lap. You pulled off a Christmas miracle. *Silo* is a go. You should be insufferably smug right now. Instead, you look like your dog just died."

I turned back to the screen, and the frozen image from inside Reeve's Textiles.

"Talk to me, Lan." His tone shifted into concern. "What happened that you aren't telling me?"

I shook my head. I couldn't put words to the colossal fuck-up of it all. If I started talking, I feared I wouldn't be able to stop.

"I think it's time you told me what happened after The Keg. What went down with August?"

His name. Hearing it spoken aloud was like getting punched in the stomach. The armor I'd so constructed around my heart over the past two weeks cracked. I squeezed my eyes shut, but I couldn't block out the image of August as I left him at the airport.

"We said goodbye," I whispered.

Felix let out a long breath. "Okay," he said softly. He waited. He was a good producer and knew when to push or when to just let the silence hang.

"I had it all." My voice threatened to break. "I

got everything I wanted. I got this movie done. Ted said yes to *Silo*. He said he didn't know I had that kind of... of emotional depth in me." I let out a harsh laugh. "And the whole time he was saying it, all I could think about was that those pages only exist because of Augie."

Felix still said nothing, but looked at me with a patient understanding.

"Thomas made me believe I couldn't have my work and a relationship."

"And then August came along," Felix finished for me.

I nodded, swallowing hard against the lump forming in my throat. "And he didn't take me away from the work. He made my work better. He was grounded and real, and he saw right through my bull- shit. Being with him, letting him in... it was the very thing my art was missing. He proved my whole goddamn theory wrong. Love isn't a liability. It's the source."

The confession hung in the air between us.

"So what happened?" Felix asked gently.

I looked away. Shame washed over me.

"Things got messy. The developer, the fight for his family's store and Main Street... it all became very real and very complicated. He retreated because he thinks it's his responsibility to fix the problem. I was stupid and tried to offer some easy Hollywood fixes instead of trying to find out what I could really do for him so he'd feel supported. I went back to trying to direct my way through a problem..."

"So call him." He made it sound so simple. "Apologize. Tell him you're an idiot."

"I don't know how," I said miserably. "The last thing I did was drive him to the airport. We said goodbye as if we barely knew each other. And I haven't heard from him since. He's in Vermont at hockey camp. I'm here. It's over."

"It's only over if you decide it is. You're a writer and a director, Lan. You don't like the ending, fix it."

"It's not a movie!" I exploded, the frustration boiling over. I stood up, pacing the small room like a caged animal. "That's the whole point! This is his life. I can't just walk back in and call 'action' and expect him to read from my new script. He explicitly told me I wasn't part of his life."

"But he is part of yours, isn't he?" Felix said, his gaze unwavering. "I'd say he's the biggest part of it right now."

I stopped in the middle of the room. He was right. In the last two weeks, Augie had become everything. The work, the success, the future I'd thought I wanted was all just a backdrop. The only thing that mattered was the cavernous space he'd left behind.

I sank back into my chair. I'd written the perfect tragedy. A man gets everything he's ever wanted, only to realize he's lost the only thing he truly needs. It was a good story. I just didn't want to be the star of it anymore.

My phone, sitting on the console, buzzed with a sudden vibration. I ignored it.

"You might want to get that." Felix looked at his phone, which vibrated in his hand. A small, wry smile played on his lips. "Speak of the devil."

I glanced at my screen. The studio's marketing department had sent a notification to the core production team. My heart gave a painful lurch.

Subject: *Teaser Trailer - 'Christmas in the Cascades' - LIVE!*

My finger trembled as I unlocked the phone. The body of the email was brief and corporate, but the words brought a mix of dread and excitement.

Team - The first teaser is now live across all platforms. Initial tracking is extremely positive. Press releases are also out, so we make the morning news cycle, first in Europe and then the U.S.

Felix cleared his throat. "Brace yourself." He sounded excited. "From the meeting I had with publicity and marketing, all signs point to this blowing up. They're projecting a huge holiday hit.

The streamer's anchoring its holiday lineup around it."

I opened the link, my heart in my throat. I hadn't seen the final trailer since it was in marketing's hands after we'd turned over the suggested footage.

The familiar studio logo flashed, followed by the swell of the Christmas score I signed off on with the composer. Then, a rapid montage of moments—the gazebo covered in twinkling lights, Brandon's character looking wistfully at the Christmas tree, Declan's character skating across the ice with a graceful confidence I knew came from Augie's coaching.

But what gutted me was the shot of Reeve's Textiles. The store glowed with warmth, every bolt of fabric and spool of thread a testament to a family's century of dedication. It was beautiful. It was magical.

And it was about to be destroyed by a developer.

I'd created the perfect advertisement for a town that was fighting for its life. I'd cast a beautiful golden light on a store that might be rubble before the movie comes out. The ultimate irony of our story —my camera had captured the very soul of what Augie was struggling to protect. Millions would see it, a memorial to what was lost.

I closed the trailer, my hand shaking. "Felix, I think I just made everything worse."

Felix looked at me, his expression unreadable. "Or, you might have handed him the solution."

I frowned, not understanding.

"The trailer isn't only a preview for a movie. It's a spotlight on Pine Ridge. On his store. On Main Street. It's exactly what you suggested he needed—publicity. A way to fight the developer with a story, not legal maneuvers. It picks up the story that Declan, Brandon, and that crowd of onlookers started telling weeks ago."

I stared at him, a dangerous hope flickering to life in my chest. "You think it could help?"

"I think you need to stop sitting here asking me questions and start asking him."

The hope sputtered and died. "He doesn't want to hear from me. He made that clear."

"Maybe," Felix acknowledged. "But if there's a chance that trailer might help him save his town, don't you think he deserves to know about it? This isn't about you anymore, Lan. It's about giving him every weapon he needs for the fight."

He was right. As usual. Even if Augie never forgave me and I never saw him again, I owed him this. I owed him every possible chance to save what mattered to him.

"Okay." I straightened my shoulders. "Okay."

Felix's phone buzzed again. His eyes widened as he read what had appeared on his screen.

"What?" A knot of dread formed in my stomach.

"Social media," he said, his voice full of disbelief. "The trailer... it's already getting traction. But not just the usual fan excitement. People are asking about the town. About the store."

He turned his phone around, showing me that the hashtag #ChristmasInTheCascades was trending, but so was something else: #FindClearwater. Viewers were trying to figure out whether the idyllic town in the trailer was a real place.

"Holy shit," I breathed. "Who is even up at this hour to start these things?"

"You know the internet never sleeps." Felix stood up, a new energy animating his tired frame. "This is what he needs, Lan. Not you apologizing. Not you suffering. He needs a story that people can get behind."

I looked back at my phone, at Augie's name in my contacts. My thumb hesitated over the call button. What if he hung up on me? What if he didn't want my help? What if it was too late?

He'd said this wasn't a narrative or a film, but the story about the town was unfolding whether he wanted it to or not.

But Felix was right. This wasn't about me. It was about Augie. About his town. About his fight. This might be exactly what the fight needed.

"Go home, Lan," he said softly. "Get some sleep. Take a shower. Then, decide what you want to do. Besides, you don't want to call him this late. It's three in the morning where he is."

I nodded, too exhausted to argue. I grabbed my phone, my keys, my jacket.

Tomorrow I'd figure out if I could bear to make the call.

NINETEEN

August

I usually loved my time in Maplewood at Ethan Gallagher's summer camp. I've done it for a couple of years now because I love the program Ethan's building.

Unfortunately, I was just marking time until I could get back to Pine Ridge to be there for Paige. We both put on a brave face when we talked. It was a small comfort that I'd be there for the vote.

I blew my whistle.

"Let's run it again!" I yelled, my voice hoarse. "Power play drill. Let's try to pick up the pace."

I watched eleven teenagers in brightly colored jerseys move with coordinated energy across the ice.

The power play drill kicked off with a five-on-four storming down the ice.

As they played, I called out suggestions.

"Cohen, keep your stick in the passing lane!"

"Martinez, eyes up, watch for the right play!"

The forwards worked the puck, moving it quickly from player to player until Galipeau, a lanky center, threaded a perfect cross-ice pass to Wilson, who one-timed it past the goalie's blocker.

"Good! That's how you collapse the defense. Wilson, excellent timing on that release. Galipeau, make sure to check all your options. You could've taken that shot."

The players gathered around me at the bench, their faces flushed with exertion. I diagrammed some options the defense had to break up that play.

My words were right and my diagrams precise, but my enthusiasm lagged behind. I did my best to keep my sadness away from the campers, though, because they deserved a solid coach who left the baggage off the ice.

The scoreboard horn sounded, signaling the end of practice.

"Good job today, everyone. Tomorrow we've got two scrimmages. Just us in the morning and then against Coach Ethan in the afternoon. I predict good things for us in the final game of the session. Get your rest tonight, and I'll see you tomorrow."

I fist-bumped many of them as they headed off the ice. Once I gathered up my extra sticks and water bottle from the bench, I followed them.

"Coach Reeve!" Wilson called out just as I exited the ice. "This is so cool! You're famous! My sister just showed me this! You're going to be in this movie?"

He handed me his phone with a social media post on the screen. It was a behind-the-scenes photo from the shoot. There I was, standing at the counter with Paige while Declan and Brandon filmed their meet-cute. The caption read: *Pine Ridge's favorite textile store along with August and Paige Reeve making a cameo in #ChristmasInTheCascades!*

This wasn't the first post people had asked me about while I'd been here. A couple of days ago, someone showed me the selfie of Declan and me at the ice rink. She wanted to know what it was like to coach an actor.

"My sister and I were just in the background, so we might get cut. We'll see what happens when it comes out in a few months."

With several players still lingering nearby, this set off a flurry of questions. I answered all of them. Their interest helped me focus on the good parts of the shoot, and not where things had ended up with the director. Even so, I was relieved when Ethan showed up and sent the kids on their way to get changed so I didn't have to talk about it anymore.

Ethan, still in his coaching gear, walked with me to the staff locker room. "Any chance I can tempt you into dinner tonight? Kyle, Dix, and Cole will all be there. Andre might make an appearance, too."

"Probably better if I pass. I'm not great company these days," I said as we entered the room and sat on opposite benches.

"You know you'll get no judgement from us if you just eat and don't talk much. We all get you've got stuff going on at home, but it might do you good to get out a little. Just being here and at the inn isn't the best way to spend two weeks."

I appreciated he was trying to be a good friend. "Can I give you a maybe?"

"I'll take that," he said as he stripped and wrapped a towel around his waist. "If nothing else, come have some pie. You love the pie... and this is the last night for you."

He had me there. "It's possible you know me too well. I'll think about it... I promise."

He gave me a nod and headed for the shower.

Before I could get undressed, my phone rang. It was a FaceTime call. Stepping out of the locker room, I crossed back into the rink, which was quiet except for the hum of the Zamboni.

I tapped "accept" before I could second guess it. Nick's smiling, easy-going face filled the screen, with Shawn peeking over his shoulder.

"Reeve!" Nick's voice boomed from the speaker. "We were starting to think you'd been abducted by bears, or a cryptid. You don't call, you don't text..."

"Time gets away during camp." I tried to sound nonchalant about it.

Shawn leaned into the frame. "Is that the official line? Because I'm sorry to say it, you look like hell. And not the hell I'm used to seeing from this one after two weeks of wrangling high schoolers."

I managed a weak smile. They were in the living room of their Boston condo. Behind them, I saw their kitchen, which brought up flashbacks of making breakfast with Landon at my place.

"Seriously, man, you okay? I know things were... rough when you left." Nick's voice was softer. His concerned expression stabbed at my heart.

Rough. That was one word for it.

"I'm hanging in there."

Shawn didn't buy it. He nudged Nick out of the frame and took the phone. "Any news on Main Street?"

I shrugged, the movement feeling heavy and

pointless. "The city council vote is still next week. We've been trying to find a way around it, but..." The words hurt me even to say. I had to swallow a lump to get the last part out. "It's over."

Shawn's face fell. "Oh, Augie. I'm so sorry."

"It's fine," I repeated, the words a hollow refrain.

"No, it's not fine," Nick's voice cut in from off-screen. "It sucks. There's got to be something to stop it. People shouldn't be able to take what's yours."

"The fight's over, Nick. It's a legal thing."

"There's always a way." Nick took the phone back from Shawn. "Look, man, I get it. You took a bad hit this summer. With the town, and... with the director. But you can't just roll over." His voice was full of the fierce, stubborn loyalty that made him a great friend and teammate. "That's not who you are. You're the guy who does what it takes to help his team win games. You don't just give up."

"This isn't a game! You think I haven't tried everything? You and Shawn, you have it all figured out, right? You make it work. The travel, the sched-ules, Shawn's deadlines, your games. It seems so damn easy."

An uncomfortable silence fell. Nick's smile vanished, and he glanced at Shawn. Not only was I too harsh, but I'd switched from talking about Pine Ridge to Landon.

"It's not easy, Augie." Shawn filled the screen again. "There's constant negotiation. Missed calls, crappy airport goodbyes and sometimes feeling like you're living on different planets. Between Nick's schedule and my deadlines, we can go three or four days where we're only communicating through brief texts. It's difficult when that happens."

He paused, his gaze steady and kind. "But it's worth it. For me, Nick's worth it. You just have to decide if the work is worth doing."

He meant for the words to be encouraging. A roadmap to a future I could still have. But all they did was illuminate the depth of my failure.

The hurt of that choice was like a gaping wound in my chest.

"I should go." I couldn't handle being confronted by my mistakes anymore. "The coaches are meeting up for dinner, and I need to get cleaned up first." It was a lie, but at least a plausible one.

"Augie, wait—"

I ended the call, cutting Shawn off. He'd been right. It was about deciding if the work was worth it. And I hadn't even been willing to try.

I grabbed my phone on the bedside table to shut off the alarm. As I silenced the noise, I saw I had a screen full of notifications.

I couldn't ignore the one on top, which had arrived after three.

Felix: *Wanted to make sure you saw the trailer.*

I clicked on the link. My thumb hovered over the play button for a long moment. Did I want to see this? To be reminded of the man that I let go?

I couldn't resist, though.

Play.

The studio logo appeared, followed by the swell of a schmaltzy, string-heavy Christmas score. A rapid-fire montage of perfect, jewel-toned moments. Declan and Brandon, looking handsome and windswept. A picturesque view of the snow-covered gazebo. A comedic beat from the awkward hockey lesson.

My heart clinched.

A shot of the interior of Reeve's Textiles filled the screen.

Goosebumps rose on my forearms.

It was our store, but it was... magical. Bathed in a warm, golden light, the bolts of fabric were an explosion of color, and the antique wooden floorboards gleamed. The camera did a slow pan across the walls of yarn, making them look like a treasure trove. The shot lingered on the red-and-black buffalo plaid flannel between Brandon and Declan. And holy shit, Paige and I were in the background.

The trailer ended with the money shot—the kiss at the gazebo, the movie title appearing in a cheerful, snowy font. *Christmas in the Cascades.*

I stared at the black screen, my heart beating fast as emotions rolled through me. I scrolled down to the comments.

Wait, where was this filmed? Is Clearwater a real place? I need to go!

It is! I was there when they were filming. The town is called Pine Ridge.

That little flannel shop is SO CUTE! I want to buy everything in it!

This looks like the perfect Xmas getaway. Booking a trip to the Cascades ASAP!

I opened the social media app I'd been avoiding. The red notification bubble was shockingly large with dozens of tags, mentions, comments. I tapped on it, bracing myself.

The first notification was from Declan, who had tagged me in a post. It was a behind-the-scenes photo I hadn't seen from the skating lesson. "Learned from the best! Thanks to the real hockey player who made me look good on skates!"

I swiped to the next one. Brandon had posted a

photo of me and him working together on his fall into Declan's arms. "Thanks for all the help @AugustReeve!"

More and more notifications appeared as I scrolled. Cast members. Crew members. People from Pine Ridge. Tourists who'd been watching the filming. All posting about the town, the movie, the experience. I'd been so wrapped up in my own misery that I'd missed the wave building online since I'd come to Vermont.

The trailer had only been out a few hours, but Pine Ridge had quickly captivated viewers. They wanted to visit and were planning holiday trips.

As I scrolled, I remembered Landon's excited voice: "This is a story, right? It's a classic David versus Goliath narrative. Small, family-owned businesses against a soulless corporate developer. People love that kind of story."

I'd shut him down. Too caught up in my own hurt and pride to hear what he was saying. But now, looking at the online reaction to just a thirty-second trailer...

Another notification popped up.

Paige: *OH MY GOD! Have you seen this?*

I opened her text to find a link to an article on a popular entertainment site: *Studio Behind "Christmas in the Cascades" Shares More About the*

Filming Location—And It's Just as Magical in Real Life!

The article featured photos of Main Street, the gazebo, and the mountains beyond. It described the "charming, historic town" and mentioned that several of the local businesses seen in the trailer were generations-old family establishments.

My pulse quickened as a line from the story jumped out at me:

"We were enchanted by Pine Ridge when we first scouted it," said Felix Barlow, the film's producer. "Fans who came to town to watch us shoot, also fell in love with it. The sad thing is this might be the only time Pine Ridge is seen on film. The town is facing development pressure that could alter its historic character, which is the very charm that drew us there in the first place. For anyone who likes what they see in the trailer, they should visit soon because we don't know how much longer the town will still look like what we captured in *Christmas in the Cascades*."

Holy shit, Felix! Had Landon put him up to that?

I went back to my social media feed searching for posts about the movie. The hashtag #ChristmasInTheCascades was trending. And then, in the replies to one post, I saw it: #SavePineRidge.

The numbness that had encased me began to crack. As I kept looking at posts and comments, my phone buzzed with new notifications every few seconds.

I returned to Landon's words, echoing in my memory with a clarity that felt like he was standing right beside me.

He hadn't been trying to direct my life. He was a master of narrative, and he had seen the story we were in. He'd tried to hand me the script for how to win.

The whole time I was seeing a fight, he was crafting a story. And stories have power.

I was a fool for not believing him.

The weight of my own stubbornness, my refusal to listen, hit me like a body check. I'd pushed him away, not just romantically but intellectually. I'd dismissed his expertise and genuine desire to help.

We'd wasted two weeks instead. We could've harnessed the momentum of the social media posts from the shoot. Was it too late now?

Another post caught my eye. This one featured a photo of Corbin Donovan, dressed in his expensive suit, standing in front of Miller's Bakery. The caption read: "Is this the villain trying to tear down the real-life Christmas movie town? #CorporateGrinch #SavePineRidge"

The trailer had unleashed a watershed of posts.

I let out a disbelieving laugh. It was the first genuine laugh I'd had in weeks. Donovan as the Grinch. It was perfect.

Maybe we could stop the vote. We were running out of time. But we still had some and we had to make the most of it.

I jumped up from the bed, my mind racing, possibilities slotting into place like a perfect power play. Donovan wanted to destroy something people were falling in love with. Landon was right. It was a story that could change everything.

My fingers flew across the screen of my phone, my hands shaking. No more sulking. No more feeling sorry for myself. It was time to fight.

But not my way. Landon's way.

I sent a quick text to Shawn.

Augie: *You're a writer. You know how to tell a story. How fast can you write me a really, really good one? About a century-old Main Street district and the town that loves it.*

His reply was almost instantaneous.

Shawn: *Whatever you need, Augie. I'm in. Tell me everything.*

There was one more thing to do. I took a deep, shuddering breath. I called Paige. She picked up on the first ring, her voice wary and tired.

"Augie? Is everything okay? It's early. I didn't expect to hear from you until you got home tonight."

"Better than okay." My voice was alive again for the first time in weeks. I was pacing my room, the frantic energy too much to contain. "That article you sent is the key. I think I have a plan. No, that's not right. I have a story."

"What are you talking about?" she asked, her voice full of confusion. "The article is great and the trailer's gorgeous. It's a wonderful way to capture a last memory of this place, but the vote is set. It's over."

"No, it's not. We've been fighting this on their terms. Legal challenges, resistance to selling. We're going to fight it on our terms now."

"What terms are those?"

"Social media. Public pressure. The internet is blowing up over the movie trailer. They want to shop at our store, everyone's store. They're already using hashtags like SavePineRidge."

"Wait, slow down—"

"Shawn's going to write something. Something that tells the real story of the store, the town, what Donovan's trying to do. Felix's comment in that article is just the beginning. We'll get it everywhere. We'll turn Donovan into the villain."

I could hear the skepticism in her silence. "Augie, I don't know—"

"I think this can work. We need to tell our truth in the right way. Make people care. Make them invested. Turn it into something bigger than just another development deal."

"How do you know this is the answer?" The faint flicker of hope in her voice made my heart happy.

"Because it was Landon's idea. He understands the power of storytelling."

Beyond rewriting the town's story, I wondered if I had the courage to reach out and ask forgiveness from the man who'd seen it first.

TWENTY

Landon

THE ROAD into Pine Ridge was a familiar winding path, but everything else had a new sheen.

Since we'd left three weeks ago at the end of production, the sleepy town had transformed into the epicenter of a cultural phenomenon. As Felix navigated the rental car down Main Street, I stared out the window at storefronts adorned with hand-painted #SavePineRidge signs. People bustled along the sidewalks—not just locals I recognized, but camera-wielding tourists snapping photos of businesses featured in the trailer.

The Pine Ridge I'd left behind was a town awaiting its execution. This Pine Ridge was alive, vibrant, and fighting back.

"Well, damn," Declan said from the backseat, his face pressed against the window like an excited child. "This is wild."

"It's amazing," Felix said.

Brandon, sitting beside Declan, snapped pictures of the scene. "Do you think this will make a difference?"

That was the million-dollar question. Felix hadn't told me about the quote he'd given for the article that ran with the trailer. He hadn't wanted to risk me talking him out of it. I hoped Augie didn't think we were going behind his back.

But then, within a day, Felix showed me posts from Augie and other Pine Ridge businesses, all using the #SavePineRidge hashtag.

I said nothing as we drove. I wasn't sure I could speak with the stress building in my chest.

"There's City Hall," Felix pointed to a stately brick building ahead, its steps crowded with people despite the late summer heat. News vans lined the curb, their satellite dishes raised to the sky.

We found parking several blocks away and headed toward the gathering. With each step, my pulse quickened. After days of strategizing with Felix, I was here not just to help save the town, but to fight for the man I loved.

If he would have me.

The silence from Augie had been deafening. Although I imagined he felt the same about me. Were we both too stubborn? Too scared? Probably both.

A familiar face broke from the crowd—Mrs. Miller, her expression a mixture of surprise and hope.

"You came." She stepped forward to meet us.

"We did," I replied.

"No matter how it all turns out, thank you for all you've done to show how wonderful Pine Ridge is. My husband and I have decided to keep the business if the vote goes the right way. We don't want to lose all that it means to us."

"Thank goodness," Declan said. "The world needs more of your cinnamon rolls."

"Right!" Brandon added. "I'm leaving here with at least a dozen."

"Come to the store when we're done here and I'll give you all you can carry." She hugged the actors.

I leaned in close to ask what I needed to know. "Is he—"

"Inside. Front row." Her eyes flickered with understanding. "It's standing room only in there. I've got someone holding chairs. I came out to find Mr. Henderson."

"How's it looking?" Felix asked, ever the pragmatist.

Mrs. Miller's mouth tightened. "We still have two of the council who'll vote to reject Donovan. Another two remain in Donovan's pocket. The mayor is waffling. I don't think he'll decide until voting time." She waved Mr. Henderson over. "We should all get inside."

I nodded, my focus narrowing to the mission at hand. "Yes. We don't want to be late."

The interior of City Hall was a pressure cooker. People packed every inch of the small chamber, and there was an anxious energy. At the front, five council members were seated on a raised dais, their expressions ranging from stoic to uncomfortable with the unprecedented attention.

And there he was.

Augie sat right where Mrs. Miller said he was, facing the council. The rigid set of his shoulders said that he was braced for whatever would happen.

I wanted to go to him, but the meeting was being called to order, and the villain of this story was stepping up to the podium.

Corbin Donovan looked different. His smug confidence held steady, but a hint of irritation cut through it. His gaze swept the room, landing briefly on the reporters and their cameras with naked disdain.

"Members of the council, I understand there's been quite a flurry over the past week with articles and social media." His voice was smooth, professional, and icy. "But I urge you to remember that municipal governance cannot be determined by hashtags and viral videos."

I felt a surge of satisfaction. He was rattled.

"Grinch. Grinch. Grinch!" A chat built up across the room and out into the hallway, which was full of people who couldn't get in.

The mayor banged their gavel and tried to call for order, but it took a moment for the chants to calm.

"We must have order," Mayor Wallace said. "We want this meeting to be an open forum, but we will clear the spectators if we have to."

The crowd murmured a bit, but settled.

"Mr. Donovan, you still have the floor."

"Thank you, Mayor Wallace. The proposal before you represents real, sustainable growth for Pine Ridge. Not the fleeting tourism of internet fame, but long-term jobs, infrastructure development, and increased tax revenue." He gestured to a sleek digital presentation being projected on screens flanking the room. "Our revised economic impact study shows a forty percent increase in permanent employment opportunities—"

"For who?" a voice called out. "Rich people you're bringing in from Seattle?"

Mayor Wallace banged his gavel. "Please hold all comments until the public portion."

Donovan smiled thinly. "As I was saying, this development represents progress. What's at stake is whether Pine Ridge will embrace the future or remain trapped in a nostalgic past that cannot sustain itself."

He continued for another ten minutes, his presentation a parade of economic projections and architectural renderings. The Pine Ridge he envisioned was unrecognizable with glass and steel uniformity. Only the mountain backdrop would remind you where you were.

When he finished, Mayor Wallace adjusted his glasses. "Thank you, Mr. Donovan. We'll now hear from those opposed to the eminent domain action."

Augie rose. My heart stuttered in my chest. He looked exhausted but determined, his brown eyes bright with purpose. He was beautiful.

"Council members." His voice was steady as he gave a nod to the five people watching him. "I could tell you about the hundred years of history you'd be erasing. I could remind you that Reeve's Textiles and many of the businesses of Main Street survived two world wars, the Great Depression, and the pandemic without asking for handouts. I could talk about the families who've built their lives around these businesses."

He gestured to the crowd behind him. "But instead, I want you to look at what's happening right now, in this community that you, and I, and many of us in this room call home. In the past month, every business on Main Street has seen record revenues."

He pulled out his phone, holding it up. "This isn't just a viral moment. It's the start of a sustainable future built on what makes Pine Ridge special. And it's the very thing Mr. Donovan wants to bulldoze and turn into a soulless structure. A place many current residents will not want to live near. As the owners of Reeve's Textiles, Paige and I are opposed to what's happening to our home, and we encourage our friends and neighbors on the council to vote no on the proposal."

For the next hour, an array of business owners and citizens spoke. They presented sales figures, showed hiring plans, and talked about bookings for the coming holiday season and even some for the following year. The momentum was building, but I saw the skepticism on the faces of two council members and the mayor. They weren't convinced this wasn't just a temporary reprieve.

My palms were sweating. Felix nudged me. "Now or never, Lan."

I stood, and the room shifted its attention. Several people recognized me, whispers rippling through the crowd. Augie, mid-conversation with Paige, turned. Our eyes met for the first time since that terrible goodbye at the airport. The shock on his face vanished, replaced by an expression I couldn't read.

I approached the podium, my heart pounding.

"My name is Landon Winslow. I directed the film that's partially responsible for the attention Pine Ridge has been receiving." Clearing my throat, I took a moment to push down the anxiety of speaking to this crowd. "Here with me are my producer and other members of the *Christmas in the Cascades* team."

I nodded to Felix, who stepped forward and placed a folder on the council table.

"Inside you'll find a formal letter of intent from Pacific Northwest Studios. Based on the record-breaking response to our trailer, they're green-lighting not just one, but three holiday films we'd like to shoot here over the next three years." I paused, letting that sink in. "Each production represents an approximate three million dollar direct investment in the local economy. That's more than was spent on the first film. Plus, it will keep this town in the hearts and minds of millions of Christmas movie fans around the world."

Murmurs swept the room. Mayor Wallace opened the folder, his eyebrows rising as he scanned the document.

"Furthermore, our stars, Declan Thorne and Brandon Atkins, are returning for all three films." I gestured to where they stood at the back of the chamber, and a ripple of excitement passed through the crowd as people recognized the actors. "Their combined social media presence reaches over five million followers, all of whom will continue to see Pine Ridge as the heart of these stories. Declan and Brandon are also willing to be a part of a Pine Ridge tourism campaign for up to the next five years."

I took a breath, shifting from business to something more personal. "When I first came to Pine Ridge, I saw it as a location. A set. But what I discovered was a community. One with a soul that can't be manufactured or replicated." My voice grew stronger. "As a filmmaker, I'm telling you that's what makes this place special and what's drawing people who saw our behind-the-scenes images and the trailer. That's also what will keep them coming.

However, that's only true if Mr. Donovan doesn't destroy the heart of the town."

I looked at Augie, whose expression had softened. "I learned from someone very important to me that authenticity isn't just a buzzword. It's the foundation for something worth fighting for."

The emotion in my voice was raw. It wasn't just the town I was talking about, and Augie knew it. I could see it in the slight tremble of his lips.

I returned my focus to the council. "If you vote for this eminent domain action, you're not just destroying buildings. You're erasing a century of history that can never be recovered. And you're guaranteeing that the economic opportunity in front of you right now will vanish. We can't shoot three movies with Donovan's structures as the backdrop. Choose Pine Ridge. The real Pine Ridge. Not some developer's futuristic version of it."

I stepped back from the podium, my legs slightly unsteady. Felix squeezed my shoulder as I passed, a silent acknowledgment of what that speech had cost me emotionally.

The hall broke out into cheers as I retreated to the rear of the chamber.

Once the mayor reestablished order, there were two hours of deliberation, questions, and legal counsel. The mayor wanted details on the studio commitment. There were questions to Donovan about his projections. They debated among themselves while we all watched, the tension almost unbearable.

Throughout it all, Augie and I kept finding each other across the crowded chamber. Each time our eyes met, goosebumps rose on my arms. I wanted to steal away with him, but we had to see the meeting through.

When the vote finally came, the room fell silent. Mark Halliday and Ana Wainright voted against the eminent domain action as expected. Mayor Wallace, looking deeply conflicted, voted for it. Marina Diaz, who had been leaning toward Donovan's side, stared at the financial projections from the studio for a long moment before voting for Donovan.

It all came down to Joseph Connor. He cleared his throat and glanced between Donovan and Augie. "My family has lived in Pine Ridge for four generations," he said slowly. "My grandfather would tell me stories about buying his first fishing rod at Henderson's Hardware, and my mom and brother shop at Reeve's every week. I have to do right by my family." He paused. "I vote no. The eminent domain action is rejected."

The room erupted. People rose to their feet, cheering and embracing. Cameras flashed. Reporters rushed forward, shouting questions. Donovan stood rigid with fury before storming out, his legal team trailing behind.

In the chaos, I lost sight of Augie. I pushed through the crowd, searching. Had he left? Had I misread everything passing between us?

Then the sea of bodies parted, and there he was, moving toward me with the same unstoppable purpose I'd seen when he coached actors how to skate. His focus was on me. The rest of the world fell away.

We met in the center of the chamber. For a heartbeat, we just stared at each other, the victory celebration swirling around us.

"You came back," he said, his voice rough with emotion.

"I never should have left you like I did."

"I shouldn't have either."

And then he pulled me to him, his hands cupping my face with a gentleness that belied his strength. The kiss was deep and desperate. I melted against him, drawing him close.

Someone wolf-whistled. To my left, I heard Paige say, "It's about damn time."

I didn't care. All that mattered was Augie.

"I'm sorry," he whispered. "I was an idiot."

"Me too. I didn't know how to just be there without trying to direct everything."

His smile was like the sunrise. "Looks as if your directing worked out pretty well."

I laughed, the sound catching on a sob of relief.

He kissed me again, softer this time.

"Hate to break up the reunion," Felix interrupted. "There are about a dozen reporters who want statements from both of you."

Augie kept his arm around me as we faced the press. We answered questions about the campaign, the movie, and the future of Pine Ridge. With each response, I felt us falling into a rhythm, a natural give-and-take, each picking up where the other left off. We were a team.

When we finally escaped the crowd, he led me to his truck. The summer evening was cooling, the golden hour casting shadows across Main Street. He drove us to his house in a silence that was charged with anticipation.

Inside, he'd barely closed the door before pulling me to him again. This kiss was hungrier, more urgent. It had been three weeks since I'd touched him. Now my hands couldn't move fast enough, tugging at his shirt, needing to feel his skin under my palms.

"I missed you," he breathed against my neck, guiding me toward the bedroom. "God, Landon, I missed you so much."

We stumbled through the doorway, a tangle of lips and hands and the frantic need to be naked and in each other's arms. I steered us, trying not to knock into the walls. My hands weren't just pulling at his clothes—they were rediscovering him, sliding his shirt from his shoulders. I nudged him back until his knees hit the edge of his bed and he tumbled onto the mattress.

The sight of him sprawled there, breathing hard, and with his gaze fixed on me was the sexiest thing I'd ever seen. It also calmed the restless anxiety I'd carried since returning to town.

"Stay," I said, the word a directive, not a request.

My fingers made quick work of the button and zipper of his jeans, peeling them down along with his briefs. His cock sprang free, thick and ready with a bead of precum glistening at the tip. The groan that tore from his throat when I wrapped my fist around him vibrated through me.

Dropping to my knees beside the bed, I never broke eye contact. My tongue swept over his cock head, earning a sharp gasp. Then I took him deep, one hand firm at the base while the other gripped his hip, holding him still. I wanted to savor Augie's hardness, the way his abs clenched, and his fingers tangled in my hair.

I dragged my lips up his length before swallowing him down again, relishing every moan and the arch of his hips. His cocked throbbed as I worked him, slow and deep.

As much as I enjoyed this, and wondered what it'd be like to have him unload in my mouth, I had a more urgent need. I pulled back, releasing him with a slick pop. His cock fell against his stomach. His gaze snapped to mine.

"Not yet." I shed the rest of my clothes quickly. He started to sit up, but I held up a hand. "I think I told you to stay." One eyebrow lifted, and he chuckled softly as he settled against the mattress.

Leaning over him, I pressed a kiss to the center of his chest before reaching for the nightstand. The lube was easy to find, right on top.

"I want you." I squeezed a generous dollop into my palm. "All of you. Now."

I poured more onto his cock, slicking him thoroughly. The groan that escaped him was pure bliss. Then I coated my entrance, two fingers working quickly in and out, preparing myself with even more urgency than I had the first time. My eyes never left his.

He nodded, a jerky movement. His hands came up, gripping my hips hard as I swung one leg over him, straddling his waist. My other hand guided him, the hot, blunt head pressing against my tight opening. As I sank down, taking him slow and deep, we both moaned loud and low.

The stretch burned for that first glorious moment, then gave way to an overwhelming fullness. His thickness stretched me perfectly. There was no barrier, just Augie, filling me.

I paused once I was seated, letting us both adjust to the intense connection. His touch slid up my thighs, then gripped my waist, thumbs digging into my hip bones. His breath came in ragged pants, eyes blazing up at me. "Oh, Landon..."

I braced my hands on his chest and moved—up, letting him almost slip out, then down, sinking back onto him with deliberate force. My rhythm was slow at first, deep rolls of my hips designed to feel every inch.

His hand caressed up to my ribs, then my shoulders, finally cradling my jaw, holding my gaze captive. The intensity in his eyes was raw, hungry need.

"Look at you," he rasped. "You're fucking beautiful like this."

The praise ignited me. I picked up the pace, rising as high as I could and driving down harder. His gasps spurred me on. My cock, hard and dripping, bounced against his stomach. I reached down, wrapping my hand around the shaft, stroking in time with my thrusts.

The sensations overloaded my senses. Each downward plunge struck deep, sending sparks of ecstasy skittering through me.

Augie trembled underneath me.

He was close. I was close.

But I held us both on the knife-edge of pleasure, my strokes becoming shorter, tighter. I maintained the punishing rhythm, denying us release, building the pressure until I saw the desperate plea in his eyes.

"Now," I choked out, as his hands gripped my hips hard. "Come with me, Augie."

That was the permission we both needed. My hand moved faster on my cock. My hips slammed down harder. He cried out, his back arching off the bed as release tore through him. I felt the hot pulse deep inside me, the intimate heat of his climax triggering mine. Thick ropes striped his chest and stomach as I ground down on him, shaking as the waves of pleasure crashed and crashed again.

My strength evaporated. I collapsed forward onto his chest, my head finding the hollow of his shoulder. He was still buried inside me as his arms encircled me, crushing me close.

For a long time, there was only the sound of our

breathing and the contentment of being exactly where we belonged. His hand traced a lazy, possessive line down my spine.

"I love you," I said, the words simple and true.

"I love you too."

He held me tighter. I was more content than I'd ever been as I surrendered to the one script I never could have written—the one where the ending was only the start of a much bigger story.

August

I woke from the best rest I'd had in weeks. My mind was still fuzzy from the sleep and the emotional whirlwind of yesterday. The council vote. The victory. Landon's return.

Landon.

I turned my head, and there he was, asleep beside me. His dark hair was sticking out in all directions, and his face relaxed in a way it rarely was when he was awake. Waking up next to him was one of the best things.

I propped myself up on an elbow and watched him.

He'd made his grand gesture—a big, cinematic moment of saving Main Street—worthy of one of his movies. But this quiet morning in my bed, with him beside me, was everything. Even if the vote hadn't gone our way, and even if he hadn't come up here to be a part of it, I'd planned to fly to LA today to find him.

Now that we knew we were going to make a future, it was time for the real work.

And for once, the idea of that work didn't scare me. It thrilled me. I was eager to discover what was next for us.

Landon stirred. For a moment, there was confusion in his blue eyes, then they focused on me, and a sleepy smile spread across his lips.

"Hey. I worried that I might have dreamed you."

"Nope." I leaned down to kiss him, a slow, deep kiss. "This is all real."

"Good," he murmured against my mouth. "Because it was a really good dream."

I pulled him to me, wrapping my arms around him, and for a long moment we took each other in as he laid his head against mine.

Landon sighed as he adjusted to look at me. "God, I love you."

His mouth crashed into mine. Our tongues slid together with a rhythm that was both new and yet had a familiarity to it.

My hands roamed down the firm planes of his

back, across his shoulders, down to his ass and back again. His fingers ran through my hair as one hand reached behind my head to bring me closer to him. The friction of skin against skin, chest to chest, sent sparks racing through me.

His cock throbbed next to mine, hard and insistent. Mine pulsed in response. He ground his hips against me, increasing the pressure through our briefs. We reacted with moans as we continued to kiss, refusing to break the connection.

Wrapping one arm securely around Landon, I flipped us over. Among the many benefits of a king-size bed was that I didn't have to worry about rolling us onto the floor. He made a grunt of surprise, but still our lips remained locked. I maneuvered so that the head of my hard dick rubbed against his shaft. He squirmed under me in response.

I couldn't take it anymore. Breaking the kiss, I pushed myself off him and sat back so I was on his legs. I pulled my cock out of my underwear and stroked it once. His mouth dropped open, and a long moan emerged. I rose to push his briefs down so they'd be out of the way.

Moving forward, I aligned myself so my cock was over his. His hard shaft bounced up and hit mine. The small bit of contact sent chills through me. I closed my right hand around us both, caressing them gently as they grew harder.

"Yes." Landon thrust into my fist and against my cock. "God, Augie, yes." He focused on me, with lust lighting up his eyes.

I leaned down slowly, bracing myself against the mattress. Landon helped by bringing a hand up to my chest for support. I brought myself back to his lips, continuing to stroke us. We were nearly the same length, though he was thicker than I was.

He gasped into my mouth as he rolled his hips, adding more to the sensations. The friction built into a delicious heat. My breath hitched as his free hand covered mine, guiding the pressure. We moved together, knowing exactly what we needed as we shuddered against each other.

I'd never been so happy to live alone and in a house rather than an apartment. Each stroke brought out loud moans from us.

"I'm not sure how much more I can take." The words came out between kisses and groans.

"Make me cum with you." He said that in a low, seductive voice I'd never heard him use. I nodded and sat up to focus on getting us off. I hated breaking the kissing, but I'd make sure it was worth it.

Landon reached up and rolled one of my nipples between his thumb and forefinger, and that sent a jolt straight to my cock. I increased the speed and tightness of my strokes. Landon was gorgeous as he fluttered his eyes closed as pleasure rippled through him.

"Fuck. This is it, Augie. I—" His words got lost in grunts and groans as cum shot from his cock and onto his chest and stomach.

That was all I needed to send me over the edge. Even as I bucked on top of him, I kept my hand moving. Some of my cum hit his chin as I unloaded.

As I slowed the pace of my strokes, he focused on me. I leaned down to lick the drop off his chin before kissing him.

"We made quite a mess," I said while keeping my face just above his.

He chuckled. "And all this before coffee."

I couldn't hold back a laugh. "Hang on a second, and I'll clean us up."

I carefully got off the bed and headed to the bathroom to get a warm cloth. Once I had taken care of the mess we'd made, I gave him a hand up.

"Alright," I said, "now on to the coffee."

I pulled on a T-shirt and sweatpants and offered Landon the same. He looked adorably rumpled in my clothes. They were too big for him and weren't black.

As we went down the hall, I hesitated at the door

to my workroom. "I want to show you something. If you want to see."

"Of course I do."

Landon followed me into the small room, and I watched his face as he took in the embroidery hoop on the central table. I'd worked daily on the project since returning from Vermont.

The town square, transformed for the movie, captured in hundreds of tiny stitches. There was the gazebo with Brandon and Declan, the large decorated tree, the extra Christmas lights, the cameras, and equipment. What had been half-finished when Landon had first seen it weeks ago was almost complete.

He stepped closer to the table. "Augie, it's beautiful."

A flush of warmth flooded me from his praise. "Working on it helped when I came back from camp. It gave me something to hold on to... I know it's not us dancing in the gazebo, but it reminds me of that."

He looked up at me, his expression full of understanding. "The night I knew I loved you."

The simple confession sent a jolt through me.

"For me too. Even if I was too scared to say it."

"At least now we've said it to each other." He gave me a soft kiss. "And I plan to say it a lot more." He kissed me again. "I love you."

We stood side by side at the table, and I leaned into him, resting my head against his.

His fingers hovered over the fabric, not quite touching. "So much detail. It's like you can see the textures."

"That's the goal. To capture not only how it looks, but how it feels."

He nodded, and I knew he understood. It was what he did with film—not just recording images, but creating feeling.

"Is that a tiny me?" He pointed to a spot near the gazebo, away from the cameras.

"It is, with the monitors. Your usual position while filming."

"Incredible." He studied it for a few more moments, taking in all the elements I tried to capture. "I can't wait to see it finished."

"You'll be the first." I hugged him, and this time I kissed him too. "Let's get that coffee."

We moved to the kitchen, the wooden floorboards cool under my bare feet. I set about making coffee, the simple, no-fuss way I always did. Landon watched with an amused expression as I put grounds in the filter, water in the machine, and pushed a button.

"Stop looking at me that way." I rolled my eyes,

but I was smiling. "Not everyone needs a Ph.D. in coffee science to start their day."

He moved to stand behind me, wrapping his arms around my waist. "When you come to LA, I'll show you what it's supposed to taste like. You'll never want to do it that way again."

The casual mention of a visit sent a wave of happiness through me. It wasn't a vague someday. It was a specific plan. A future we were building.

Once the coffee was ready—perfectly drinkable, despite Landon's grimace at his first sip—we settled at my small kitchen table.

"So, let's figure this out." I set my mug down with a dramatic thump.

Landon raised an eyebrow. "Figure what out?"

"Us." I pulled out my phone and gestured for him to do the same. I placed them side by side in front of us—two black rectangles containing our chaotic schedules. "I have to be in Denver for training camp in two weeks. You've got *Silo* prep coming up, right?"

A serious, focused look replaced his easy morning smile as he nodded. The director was back, ready to make a plan.

"My work on *Cascades* is basically done. The things that are left are ones I'll just have to review and approve." His voice took on the precise cadence he used when planning a shot. "*Silo* prep will go for ten to twelve weeks. There'll be some time off for the holidays in there. Then eight weeks of shooting, mostly in California, but there'll be some location work wherever we shoot the exteriors. And there'll be a long post-production process."

"Okay." I pulled up my calendar, which was loaded with the upcoming season details, which had come out while I was in Vermont. "So, I've got two weeks before training camp starts. And you're here now."

"Two weeks," he echoed, a promise in his voice.

"And I thought..." I took a breath, my pulse quickening with the idea. "What if I was in LA with you until it's time to go to Denver? You can show me your life there, just like you've seen mine here."

His eyes lit up as a smile spread across his face. "Yes. Absolutely yes."

"Once the season starts, it's a beast." I pointed at the calendar, the long stretch of games, back-to-backs, road trips that lasted nearly two weeks in some cases. The old me would have seen this as proof that we'd never be able to make anything work. The new me saw it as a a problem to be solved.

"But, in a couple of months—" I swiped to what I wanted him to see—"there's a five-game homestand in Denver in November. Twelve straight days where

I'm sleeping in my own bed." I looked at him, my heart pounding with hope. "You could come to Denver."

His fingers flew across his phone screen, checking his schedule. "I could. We'll be in pre-production then. I know Felix and I could make that work." His excitement was palpable. "I assume you'll have practices at least some of those days too."

I grinned and nodded, a burst of joy spreading through me as he marked the time on his calendar. It wasn't a vague "we'll make it work." It was almost two full weeks. A specific time frame. It was real.

We spent the next hour hunched over our phones. It was the most romantic thing we'd ever done, even more profound than any grand declaration or even the sex. This was our blueprint for the future, and we were building it together.

After we'd gone through what we could, I took his hand. "It's going to be hard." I stated what we both knew. "There are going to be times when it just sucks. When one of us has a bad day and the other is a thousand miles away."

"I know." He squeezed my hand. "But it won't suck as much as the last three weeks did. Nothing could suck that much."

He was right. The hollow ache of his absence

was the alternative. And I wasn't willing to accept that.

We booked the flights right then. My flight back to LA with him. His flight to Denver in November. A weekend trip to Denver for him in February. The confirmation emails pinged in our inboxes, digital proof of our commitment. We also marked our calendars for games I had in LA and Anaheim since we could see each other while I was there.

The man who had walked into the store a few weeks ago, the man I'd danced with in the town gazebo, wasn't the same man I'd left at the airport.

We'd become each other's home.

"I love you," I said, the words simple and true.

His smile was everything. "I love you too."

EPILOGUE

Landon
December

THE LAST TIME I was in Seattle with Augie, it ended with a terrible airport goodbye that never should've happened.

Today I sat in the Seattle Riptide's arena, watching the Denver Mountaineers battle it out. The score was 1-1 with a couple of minutes left to go. I was on the edge of my seat. Despite being in enemy territory, I proudly wore Augie's jersey.

I'd become an instant hockey convert during the two weeks I spent with Augie in Denver. Watching on TV was fine, but being in the arena brought the game to another level. It was impossible not to be swept up in the speed and skill, especially watching the man I loved play. I also got an education about the sport sitting with the partners and spouses of the Mountaineers' players, who welcomed me to their group.

That trip had been everything we'd hoped. I'd worked from his condo, gone to every home game, and learned more about him. In so many ways, it mirrored the days he'd spent with me in LA after Pine Ridge's future was secured.

Sometimes we went out. More often, however, we stayed in.

My attention snapped back to the game. An off-sides call on Seattle brought play to a stop, and the face-off was set in the neutral zone. Denver swapped lines, and Augie was back on the ice. Denver's center won the face-off, sliding the puck to the right wing, who sent it to Augie. He skated backwards, checking his options, acting like there was no pressure from Seattle's players.

He fired a pass up to the center breaking open through traffic. The Mountaineers surged forward in a coordinated rush. Just before a Riptide defenseman could close the gap, the puck snapped back to Augie in a blind return pass. He barely held it for a second before threading it to the wing, who didn't hesitate in taking a shot.

The shot flew past the goalie, and the red light flared to life behind the net.

I jumped from my seat and cheered along with the other Denver fans in the arena.

There were only twenty seconds left. Seattle gave it everything they had, but Denver held the line and took the win.

As the crowd exited, I followed the directions I'd been given to reach the VIP lounge where I'd meet Augie. Tugging the lanyard from under my jersey, I flashed the credential as I made my way through the maze of concrete corridors.

I'd been to enough games to know I might weight a while, but only thirty minutes later he arrived.

Fresh from the shower, Augie's hair still curled damply at the edges. He wore a dark coat over his travel suit and wheeled his luggage beside him. His gaze found me instantly as if he'd known exactly where I'd be.

There was no dramatic sprint, no movie-style embrace—just that invisible pull that always drew us together when we were in the same room. When he reached me, he opened his arms. I stepped into them and we enveloped each other in hugs.

"It's good to see you," he said, his voice rough but warm against my ear.

I looked up at him, smiling. "You too."

It'd only been three weeks since I'd been in Denver, but nothing beat seeing Augie in person. Phone screens didn't do him justice.

He leaned in, kissing me slow and deep. It wasn't too much for a public display, but it was exactly the reconnection I needed.

When we finally broke apart, I rested my forehead against his. "Let's get out of here."

"We need to wait—"

"Hey, sorry I wasn't faster." I turned to see a man I didn't recognize. "I hope I didn't hold you up."

"It's all good." Augie fist-bumped him. "Ethan, this is my boyfriend, Landon. Landon, this is Ethan." Augie lowered his voice. "He plays for the enemy."

"But also the guy who runs the hockey camp." I made my hand into a fist, and Ethan bumped it. I'd learned during the Denver trip this was the preferred handshake for hockey players. "It's great to meet you."

"You too. Congratulations on the movie, and on getting together." Ethan clapped Augie on the shoulder. "It's good to see this one so happy."

A faint blush rose in Augie's cheeks, which was always an adorable look.

"Anyway, I just wanted to say hello. If we ever land in the same city, Andre and I would love to get dinner with you."

"You're welcome to come to Pine Ridge for the premiere tonight," Augie said. "Hang out after."

Ethan shook his head. "Appreciate the invite, but Andre gets in around eight, so I'm cooking and then we're crashing."

"Totally understand," I said. "We'll make it happen sometime."

"For sure. You guys should get going. Can't have you late for your own movie." Instead of fist bumps, there were hugs for both of us. "See you soon. And Reeve, we'll be coming for revenge in January."

"Bring it, Gallagher."

They laughed, and we all headed out of the lounge. Ethan went a different direction, probably back to the locker room, and we left through the players' exit. Augie's hand found mine as we walked past staff members and players who were also leaving.

"You played great," I said as we stepped into the brisk air outside the arena. "That last goal was incredible."

"Yeah. The setup for that couldn't have gone better. We all did what we were supposed to."

Augie never bragged about his part in a game. He didn't have to.

"How'd the audition go this morning?" Augie asked from the passenger seat as we made the drive to Pine Ridge.

I stole a quick glance at him and smiled. "Fantastic. We found our Sarah. Emma Sloane is incredible. Has this intensity that's perfect for the role."

"That's huge!" He reached over and squeezed my knee. "I'm so glad she said yes. She was so good in the movie we watched last week."

Every night, no matter where we were, we made time for a video call. Sometimes it was a sleepy good-night after a late game. Other times, we'd talk for hours. We even watched movies together over Face-Time. There were always texts, photos, and random "thinking of you" calls that came out of nowhere.

We kept showing up for each other. And it worked.

"Still looking for your John, though?"

"Yeah. It has to be the right person. Someone who can embody that stoic determination but with cracks showing through." I looked at him, at his strong profile against the winter landscape. "Someone a little like you, actually."

He laughed, a warm sound that filled the car. "I'm no actor."

"No," I agreed, "but your type is everything I'm looking for."

As we neared Pine Ridge, I saw new things. The signs for the "Cascade Loop Scenic Byway" now had smaller brown signs underneath them pointing the way to the "Historic Pine Ridge Town Center."

When we crested the hill overlooking the valley, the town came into view. "Wow."

It wasn't the artificial Christmas-in-July town I'd created. This was the real thing. Wreaths with big red bows hung from every lamppost, and strings of colored lights stretched across Main Street, twinkling in the winter dusk. At the heart of it all, a massive pine tree towered over the town square, its star brushing the sky.

But it wasn't just the decorations. It was the people. The sidewalks bustled with people in scarves and hats, arms full of shopping bags, ducking in and out of stores. There were locals I recognized. More importantly, there were also tourists.

"Augie, it's..." The words caught in my throat as awe washed over me.

"Yeah." The note of pride in his voice didn't escape me. "It's been busy since the film wrapped and the trailer dropped. But since Thanksgiving, it's been unlike anything anyone in town has seen before. Paige hired three more people for the holiday season."

"What about Mrs. Miller?" I remembered her

hesitation during the summer, her fatigue, and readiness to retire.

"Thriving." Augie's smile was wide. "The bakery's become a destination. She and Frank hired a manager so they can have more time away. She's also mentoring two local kids who want to learn the baking business. And Frank is recovering well from his knee replacement."

He turned onto Main Street, and it was like driving through the idealized version of the town I had tried to create on film. Every storefront was decked out, even more lavishly than in the movie. The marquee of the old movie theater was lit up, its letters spelling out:

TONIGHT: PINE RIDGE PREMIERE - CHRISTMAS IN THE CASCADES - 8 PM

"New businesses too." Augie pointed out the window. "A couple from Seattle opened a coffee shop next door to the bakery. They're already talking about knocking down the wall to make one big space. There's an outdoor gear store focusing on sustainable products, and a craft brewery opens next week."

I parked in front of Reeve's Textiles. My heart gave a familiar thump. I looked at the store where we had first met, where we'd clashed and sparked and started this impossible love story. The front window was a masterpiece of holiday cheer. A vintage wooden sled was propped up, surrounded by bolts of rich red and green fabric, knitted stockings, and artfully arranged skeins of yarn that looked like colorful snowballs. A small, elegant sign hung in the window: *As Seen in the Motion Picture Christmas in the Cascades.*

"Come on," Augie said, squeezing my hand before he let go. "Someone's wanting to say hello."

We walked into the store, and a small bell chimed over the door. Customers milled about, their arms laden with yarn, fabric, and crafts from the local artisans' display.

Paige Reeve was a different woman. The exhausted, frayed-at-the-edges warrior from the summer was gone. Her hair was down, her eyes were bright, and she was laughing—a sound I'd never heard from her before. When she looked up and saw us, her entire face lit with joy.

"They're here, Rose!" Paige set down her cutting shears and came around the table. To my surprise, she pulled me into a warm, firm hug. "Landon. It's good to see you."

"You too, Paige. The place looks... incredible."

"It's been the best kind of chaos. We sold out of that buffalo plaid from the movie four times already. I'm thinking of naming it *The Winslow.*"

I laughed, heat creeping up my neck. "Please don't."

Augie put an arm around my shoulders. "Paige, be nice. He's my guest."

"Is he?" Her eyes twinkled as she looked between us. "I think he's more like family now." She embraced her brother and kissed him on the cheek.

"Uncle Augie!" Rose's voice rang out before she came into view. "Uncle Landon!" She tore around the corner, barreling straight toward us. She crashed into Augie first, hugging him tight. "Merry Christmas!" Then she came to me, and I knelt to hug her.

"Merry Christmas to you," I said as I released her.

"Did you see everything at the theater?" The excitement in her voice was contagious. "The plaid carpet is so cool."

"Not yet," Augie said, ruffling her hair. "We'll see it tonight."

"Speaking of, you two better get going." Paige glanced at the clock on the wall. "You need to get ready."

"And so do we," Rose added.

Back at Augie's house, we changed into black suits with white shirts. Augie had a deep red tie, while I wore a dark green one. A nod to the festive occasion. Before we left, he brought me to the kitchen, where a small wrapped package with a plaid bow sat on the kitchen counter.

"What's this?" I asked, tracing the edge of the plaid bow.

"Something for you." He shrugged, a hint of nervousness creeping into his voice. "Something between an early Christmas gift and celebrating the movie's opening. Go on, open it."

I unwrapped the package, folding back the tissue paper to reveal something flat, framed in simple black wood. When I turned it over, my breath caught.

It was the embroidery of the town square. It was complete, every detail perfect. In the corner, he'd stitched the initials "AR + LW."

"Augie, it's beautiful." I ran my finger along the edge of the frame.

"I thought it'd be nice for your office. So you'd always have a piece of here with you."

It was such a simple gesture, but it undid me. A piece of here with me, a piece of him, of us, of this town that had helped bring us together.

"But why did you sign both of us?" I pointed at the initials.

"Because without you, that scene would've never existed." He pulled me close, and I set the frame aside so I could embrace him properly.

"I love it," I said, my voice breaking. "I love you."

His smile lit up the room. "I love you too."

THE PREMIERE WAS the most charmingly small-town event I'd ever seen. The sidewalk outside the theater was roped off, a twenty-foot strip of plaid carpet—the same pattern Julian and Callum met over—rolled out. A photographer from the high school paper snapped pictures beside a reporter from an entertainment magazine that had scored exclusive national coverage.

Augie held my hand as we walked the short carpet, stopping to greet people he knew. He looked effortlessly handsome, and pride swelled in my chest until it was almost too much.

"Landon! Augie!" Mrs. Miller called, waving from near the theater entrance. She hurried over with Frank beside her, cane in hand but moving more easily than I remembered. "I hear you two have to leave early in the morning. Stop by on your way out, and there'll be cinnamon rolls for you both."

"That's so nice of you." I was touched she'd remembered my sweet tooth. "But are you sure? We're leaving around five."

"Oh, we'll be baking by then. Just knock on the door. The crew knows you'll be stopping by."

"Thank you so much."

She pulled me into a hug, which meant the world. Augie got one too.

Inside, the theater was a restored single-screen palace from the 1940s, all plush red velvet seats and ornate gold trim. The air smelled of buttered popcorn and peppermint. Every seat was taken, the audience buzzing with anticipation.

Felix found us near the front and waved us over to the two seats he'd saved. He greeted me with a bear hug, his eyes shining. "Look at this, Landon," he said, gesturing around the excited scene. "You did this."

"I had help," I said, looking at Augie.

"That you did," Felix agreed, clapping Augie on the shoulder.

We settled in near the front. Shawn sat beside Felix, practically glowing with excitement even though Nick couldn't make it due to a game on the East Coast. Declan and Brandon were behind us—

and holding hands. I'd have to ask about that later. Paige and Rose sat next next to them.

"How's the Denver-LA thing going?" Shawn asked.

"It's been fine," I confirmed. "But we're done with that."

Augie's hand found mine. "Landon's heading back to Denver from here to finish *Silo* pre-production before location shooting starts. Denver's going to be his home base."

Shawn's eyebrows shot up. "Really?"

Felix simply smiled since he already knew about the plan.

I shrugged, trying to look nonchalant. "I even found a great office space I can work out of, so I don't turn Augie's guest room into utter chaos."

"And when he's in Pine Ridge, we're going to set up the space over the store so he can work."

"Congrats. That's awesome," Declan said. He and Brandon hugged us from behind.

We'd both loved the time we'd spent together in LA and Denver, but we missed each other when we were apart. One late-night call when Augie was exhausted after a brutal overtime game was all it took for me to suggest moving there.

"Home isn't a place," I'd told him, echoing the movie's cheesy line but meaning it with every fiber of my being. "It's you. And I want to be with you as much as possible."

And just like that, we decided I'd go from the premiere to Denver. There was no reason I couldn't live either in Pine Ridge or in Denver and travel when I needed to.

The lights dimmed, and cheers erupted from the crowd as the studio logo appeared on-screen, followed by the familiar swell of the Christmas score.

I watched the movie with a mix of professional detachment and pride, knowing what it all meant to this town. I saw my shots, my lighting choices, the edits I'd agonized over.

The audience laughed and sighed in all the right places, and that told me I'd done my job. Hearing their reactions was everything. I rarely watched my films with anyone outside the industry, but I had goosebumps sitting with this crowd, who were so integral to the vibe the movie had.

I looked over at Augie, his face illuminated by the flickering light, a small smile curving his lips. He didn't need to say a word. He already knew the difference between what was real and what was fake. The most powerful scenes of the summer had happened when the cameras weren't rolling.

On screen, the movie reached its climax. Declan as Callum, delivering Shawn's heartfelt speech in the gazebo. "Home isn't a place," he said, his voice full of perfectly calibrated emotion. "It's a person."

Behind me, someone kissed and there was a small sign of containment. I suspected I knew who that was.

And then Augie's fingers closed around my hand in the dark. It was a quiet affirmation in the face of the grand gesture on the screen.

Besides moving to Denver, Augie had the All-Star break coming up. We planned to meet in New Mexico at a cabin in the mountains, halfway between his commitments in Phoenix and my set in Texas. I'd go to his All-Star events, and he'd come to set.

We were mapping a life together, one day, one call, one conversation at a time.

The fictional couple got their scripted kiss under the fake snow, and the credits rolled. The audience burst into applause as the lights came up.

But I didn't focus on the audience. I leaned over and kissed the very real man beside me, my heart full. It was better than any movie ending could ever be.

AUTHOR'S NOTE

I love Christmas movies.

Bring on the holiday films that start airing 24/7 even before Halloween! If I need comfort programming, I'll watch them any time of year. The same goes for holiday-themed books—sometimes those cozy vibes are exactly what I need.

Romance plus holiday magic plus saving something (a store, a town, a ranch, a community center, etc.) is absolute catnip for me.

While I've written a few holiday stories over the years (*Rivals, Room Service, Taking a Shot at Love*), this is my first full-length Christmas novel.

I've been thinking about this story since spring 2020. It was supposed to be the next book after *Keeping Kyle,* but I couldn't quite land on the right scenario.

I knew I wanted a hockey player and a director to fall in love. I knew it would be a holiday story set in the summer during the filming of a Christmas movie.

But there were big questions.

First, what did hockey player Augie need to save? I went through several ideas before landing on the combination of his family's store and other Pine Ridge businesses. What that store was changed multiple times, too. I also wanted Augie to be an artist, and eventually the idea of a textile shop clicked. It gave Augie a creative, crafty outlet and set up the perfect meet-cute for the movie-within-the-book.

Then there was movie director Landon. For a while, I toyed with making this a second-chance romance, but I never found a backstory that felt right. Switching to opposites attract—with just a hint of enemies to lovers—made everything snap into place.

I also had a blast coming up with the fictional movie: the meet-cute in the shop, the snowed-in decorating scene, the grand gesture at the gazebo. All things that I love.

It may have taken five years to figure out this book, but I'm thrilled with how Augie and Landon's story developed.

Writing it in 2025 also gave me the chance to connect the movie's script to romance author Shawn Kendrick, who was introduced in *The Hockey Player's Snow Day*. Since Shawn and his boyfriend Nick also appear in *Pride by the Book*, it was perfect to slip in a line that Shawn would be on set during filming. Having Shawn and Nick be a part of this story was incredibly fun.

Since this book is about a Christmas movie, I couldn't end this note without sharing my favorites. These are my personal top five—which means they're Augie's favorites too:

#1: The *Christmas in Evergreen* series. These four movies from the Hallmark Channel (2017–2020) are set in a picture-perfect small town filled with community, heartfelt wishes, a dash of magic, and plenty of *save the thing* energy. Augie even thinks about this series in Chapter 5.

#2: *The Christmas Setup*. Lifetime's 2020 film is the first holiday movie from a major network featuring a gay couple as the leads. Real-life husbands Blake Lee and Ben Lewis star in this sweet, charming, matchmaking-mom, second-chance romance with a *save the historic train station* plotline.

#3: *A Very Nutty Christmas*. A 2018 Lifetime movie where Barry Watson plays Chip, a nutcracker prince come to life. He helps overworked bakery owner Kate, played by Melissa Joan Hart, rediscover her Christmas spirit. I love the magical element in this story—similar to my love of the wish-granting snowglobe in the *Evergreen* movies.

#4: *Dashing in December*. Paramount Network's 2020 gay holiday romance, built on save-the-ranch stakes and delicious enemies-to-lovers energy. Peter Porte and Juan Pablo Di Pace are terrific in it.

#5: *The Holiday Sitter*. Jonathan Bennett and George Krissa star in Hallmark's 2022 gay Christmas movie. Jonathan is a work-obsessed bachelor who gets called on to babysit his niece and nephew. Luckily, George is across the street to help... and of course, feelings happen. Honorable mention goes to Jonathan's *The Christmas House* movies, where he plays one half of a married couple.

Thanks for reading *A Very Merry Movie in Pine Ridge*. I hope you enjoyed Augie and Landon's journey as much as I loved writing it.

Huge thanks to my husband—and fellow Christmas movie enthusiast—Will, who listened to me talk about this book for years and was an amazing beta reader. Will also writes as William Gayheart, and you should absolutely check out his holiday romance *His Big Holiday Firefighter*—a charming story about a baker and a firefighter—available wherever you buy ebooks.

Whether you're reading this book during the holiday season, during Christmas in July, or at any other time of year. I hope it gave you all the cozy holiday vibes.

-Jeff
December 2025

Hockey Hearts **Romance Series**

- *The Hockey Player's Heart* (co-written with Will Knauss)
- *The Hockey Player's Snow Day*
- *Keeping Kyle* (A Hockey Allies Bachelor Bid Romance)
- *Head in the Game*
- *Rivals*
- *Taking a Shot at Love*
- *Skating Back to You* (A Hockey Hearts and On Stage crossover)
- *Checked by His Teammate* (part of the Bennett Brothers Duology)
- *Pride by the Book* (A Love in Maplewood Romance)
- *A Very Merry Movie in Pine Ridge*

On Stage **Romance Series**

- *Dancing for Him*
- *Love's Opening Night*

More Romance

- *Bicycle Built for Two*
- *Room Service*
- *Somewhere on Mackinac*
- *Summer Heat*
- *Their Four Date Experiment* (co-written with William Gayheart)

Young Adult Titles

Codename: Winger series

Available in ebook, paperback, and audiobook (narrated by Kirt Graves).

- *Tracker Hacker* (includes the bonus short story *A Very Winger Christmas*)
- *Schooled*
- *Audio Assault*
- *Netminder*

More Young Adult

Available in ebook, paperback, and audiobook (narrated by Jason Frazier)

- *Flipping for Him*

Non-Fiction

- *Content for Everyone: A Practical Guide for Creative Entrepreneurs to Produce Accessible and Usable Web Content* (co-written with Michele Lucchini)

ABOUT JEFF

Jeff Adams writes queer romance and young adult fiction—often with a hockey player (or two) at the heart of the story. He's been telling stories since middle school and became a published author in 2009.

Jeff lives in central California with his husband of 25+ years, Will (who writes as William Gayheart). He loves musicals, both the Red Wings and Penguins hockey teams, and reading (of course).

In his day job, he's a digital accessibility expert, helping companies build more inclusive online experiences. He's also the co-author of *Content for Everyone*, a guide for creatives who want to make their content accessible.

Find Jeff's books and join his newsletter—where you'll get a free *Hockey Hearts* novella—at Jeff AdamsWrites.com.

9 798999 144232